The City Of Roses Series

Book 1 Dead Roses

Chapter One

2005

15-year-old Tia Brandt, gazed at the blood

trickling down her mothers forearm. As the syringe

lay next to, the long time heroin addict Nyemiah.

Her eyes rolled into the back of her head. The

color of a blue sky, with foggy gray contrast. Tia

knew her mother had succeeded, in suicide from

the demon she loved greatly. Nyemiah was a closet

heroin addict. Who portrayed herself as a vixen.

Prostituting from the age of 12. She was far from game goofy.

1989.

Nyemiah Gave birth to Tia when she was only 13 years old. The public eye would have thought she was a grown woman, however she was just a baby in the game. With beautiful caramel skin, green almond shaped eyes to be exact, medium length hair, that she wore in a Doobie wrap. Nyemiah had DD breast and an ass that could stop traffic. She looked to be in her early 20s', however she was just a child. 12 years old when she, met

3

her babies father/pimp. D-Loc was a 26-year-old member of the Rolling 60 crip gang. With his charm and his good looks he quickly swept Nyemiah off her feet,and right onto the track.

D-Loc was 6'3 With chocolate skin, slanted eyes, and a mouthful of gold. He was handsome like a male model ,he knew at a young age that his looks would make other niggas think he was a sucka. Which made him take on the role of an alpha male. At the age of 11 D-Loc picked up a blue flag, a 9mm pistol getting put on to The 60s' Crip Gang. To claim his dominance. At 13 he was caught slipping with, A pistol and a quote of crack cocaine. D-Loc already been in and out of Juvie.

The gun charge as well as a dope charge put the non-snitching teenager away for a year. D-Loc paroled close to his 15th birthday finding himself, with a child on the way. By his first baby's mother Latasha. She was a 20-year-old veteran hoe by then. She introduced him to the pimp game. By the time the D-Loc was 18 he was in and out of Portland with a stable of 8 to 10 hoes. They were all bad bitches. Latasha was brutally murdered in Las Vegas Nevada by a trick when she was 21. D-Loc was furious and depressed, he didn't know how he could go back to his hometown, and tell his then one year-old son that his mother was, dead. Without Latasha around to keep the other hoes in line. It was as if all the bitches thought they could pull one over on a 20 year old D-Loc. The nigga was still a gangster so he introduced the hoes to his pimp hand. Beating them relentlessly whenever they stepped out of line. When Nyemiah fell into his lap, he knew after eight long years he found himself a new bottom bitch to hold shit down. Nyemiah was fast at a young age. It was the year 1989 when she met D-Loc. She craved being around the Crips. Especially the flyest Crip of her era, D-Loc.His name was buzzing in the hood for making gwap.She heard the rumors of him being a pimp, however she wasn't concerned with how he got his money. She just wanted to live the life of a ghetto fabulous queen. Coming from a home of a father who died in the Vietnam war and a crack addicted mother Nyemiah feigned for a savior. D-Loc had became ruthless after Latasha's death. If there was any bitch in his presence, she was either from Rollin 60s' Crip ,or paying his pockets. When he saw Nyemiahs' shapely body approaching him on Union Avenue. He knew he would knock her. At first glance he guessed the caramel beauty to be 18 or 19 years old. He didn't discover her real age until a few years down the line. She was only 12 years old. Attending Harriet Tubman middle school. Her age would have stopped the entire situation from occurring. She quickly lied to him at their first meeting, telling him she was 17 years old. Dloc tested her young pussy out. She has started fucking a year before. So she wasn't shy; he quickly put her on the blade nationwide. Making A fortune from her striking good looks. Nyemiah cared for D-Loc and his son Martron in the best way. She was still young, yet she lead a grown woman's life. She Prostituted up into her seventh month of pregnancy with Tia having her child never slowed her down it just made her grind harder. D-Loc was physically abusive to her; they split up when she was 19. Stay-Clean was Nyemiahs' "Captain save a hoe". She soon took over Stay-Cleans stable due to him being murdered in a dice game. The only thing she did not like about his operation was. He kept his bitches in Portland. Nyemiah took her hoes across country with an escort service like Dloc had taught her. Tia lived with her mother,who was still addicted to crack cocaine. Nyemiah found her own demon at the age of 22. She has so much pain in her young life that she decided to snort cocaine on a trip to New York. She was at a well-known club celebrating with her bitches when she tried white china heroine. She soon couldn't get the monkey off our back. The only way she knew how to support her habit Was Saling pussy. Her stable soon fell apart there was no organization, there was no direction. No one in Portland knew why Nyemiah was a veteran hoe with a stable. She suddenly was back on the stroll herself . She never lost her looks, she kept her addiction hidden from Dloc as well as her cohorts in Portland but Tia knew her mothers secret.

Back to reality

Tia kneeled over her dead mother crying.Tears of anger. Regarding how selfish her mother had always been. Lying there dead at 29 years old. Tias' pink Juicy Couture Valor suit top, was drenched in tears. Even through the thick tears her she was still very beautiful. She had her fathers chocolate skin tone, long thick black hair, with her mothers striking figure and captivating green eyes. Tia was definitely beautiful. She dialed 911 the ambulance rushed to their plush condo located in Vancouver Washington. Nyemiah was big on living in the cut. The lifestyle she lived required laying low you never shit where you sleep.The police and medics were shocked at how lavish their home was. French Decor, white leather sofas, large flat screen televisions in each room.Multiple paintings, sculptures and beautiful photos of both mother and daughter everywhere they turned. It was shocking to put the beautiful woman in a body bag. The police asked Tia of any relatives she had? Tia knew her father usually had warrants for his arrest, her granny had died a year prior. The only person she could think to call was her older brother Martron.

"Hey bro what's good? Nothing sis what you been up to?" She was soon swept by tears. "Martron mom is dead, I came out of my bedroom to get something to drink and I found her, be real Tia! Nye cannot be gone. Did you call dad? No I need you to come swoop me the police are here. It ain't cool bro. Martron was game tight he knew Tias spoke in code. He was her only option. He sped on the 205 freeway, he had merged from N.E Sandy Blvd. It was ironic how he was in some fire pussy when he had to heard that deadly news.

Martron was only a few years behind Nyemiah. He was a 24 year old gangster in his own right. He was from LOP, the Locked Out Piru gang originated in Portland . Every one from Portland, knew him as Mar-Ru. He was a splitting image of his father, however he was fascinated with the Pirus. Martron hated D-Loc because of Latasha's death. He didn't discover the hate until he was 10 years old. When Nyemiah the only true person in his life at the time.Told him the truth. By the age of 13 He had a red flag out of the right pants pocket, Claiming L.O.P. He drove quickly and his 7.45 BMW on the freeway, crying furiously, dressed in all black ready for war.

His first thought was Nyemiah had been murdered. He listened to sad tunes, he hated D-Loc more then ever. Feeling a sudden urge to kill the man he felt, destroyed so many lives. When Martron saw the flashing red and blue light of the Ambulance truck. He knew the death was real reality struck him quickly.Tia rushed out to her brother latching onto his black T-shirt in Urgency. Martron escorted Tia Into the condo. She packed the majority of her clothing in both her and her mothers Gucci luggage.Tia moved fast, neither her or Martron wanted to be questioned. She had barley spoke to the on scene detective that questioned her. They left the condo in a haste.

The foreign car glided on the highway Tia sat silent. "Hey Tia talk to me. Was somebody in there with y'all? Don't just sit there please tell me baby girl. It was just me and mom. She's been fucking with that black for a while now. Does our punk ass dad know this."Martron asked while he punched the steering wheel with anger. "No he never knew she fucked with that shit, he only came over sometime to visit and check traps." Tia finished her last words with tears streaming down her face. Martron do you got some dro?" Martron was a street nigga. He participated in a lot of illegal activity. Including smoking weed. He viewed Tia as a baby born into a horrible genetic pool. His usual behavior was to shelter her from drugs, or

gang banging. Instead of shielding her, he passed

a pre-rolled blunt to his little sister to light. "Do

you want me to get us a room tonight ? You know

niggas be on my head, plus a gang of bullshit at

my house, I promise I'm a get us a place." Martron

was a businessman he had two babies mothers that

lived lavishly. Zayley in Portland and Monica in

California his apartment was not a place he would

subject Tia to his blood homeboys and drug

dealers were there. He did not want his little sister

exposed to the environment. Tia knew her brother

was going to come through with finding a place

for them to stay.She knew he sold major weight as

well. He wasn't only a force to be reckon with on the street he was a businessman with a lucrative Columbian connect. He had unlimited access to both cocaine and heroine.He owned a laundry mat in North Portland, a car mechanic shop, and two hair salons in Northeast Portland. He laundered his drug money through his business'.

Tias' mother had been valuable for most of her material needs. But her big brother bought her expensive designer clothes. The majority of the young women attending Jefferson high school could not afford The clothing Tia wore. He drove from Portland to Vancouver Washington faithfully in one of his many European cars to pick her up for school every day. The high schoolers would look in awe when Martrons vehicles pulled up in front of the high school. He had a red 500 series class Mercedes Benz, A black 7.45 Beemer, Cream Range Rover with 28 Inch rims. Martrons favorite car was his money green Bentley. The vehicle cost more than a year's worth of a hard workers salary.

Tia was a square, but she still loved the attention at school. Seeing her mother dead made the ride from Vancouver to Portland feel like a blur.

"Martron can you pick up Cynthia so she can stay the night with me please? Tia you know that little bitch a brand I'm sorry Cynthia is to much. Please Martron?"

 Tia asked in a begging tone of voice. "OK only this one time blood." Being a nigga with a reputation had perks and consequences. Most of Martrons family was from Rolling 60s' and he was their rival. Martron knew Cynthia was from Kirby block Crips. He hated Tia hanging around the hood rat. He viewed Cynthia as a set up artist, befriending his sister because,she had money and clout. He believed Cynthia constantly tried to influence his sister to have sex and gang bang. Tia had a mind of her own and college was in her near future. Maintaining a 4.0 GPA she put school first.Cynthia was was her best friend, someone she viewed as loyal and down to earth.

Martron pulled up to Cynthias ran down house three blocks away from Jefferson high school. He felt out of place parked in his flashy well-known car in the crip neighborhood. Cynthia received a text from Tia when they were on their way she ran to the car to console her friend. "Who did it cuz who? Bitch hop in the car, or get left crab! you better be lucky my sister sick right now or we wouldn't be here you crab ass bitch. And you better not tell nobody where we're going !" Cynthia fell silent ,she got into the backseat dressed in a Kansas City Royals hat a long hair weave flowed to her ass. A tight royal blue flannel stretched across her enormous breast. Cynthia was clad in Seven jeans and blue timberland boots to complete her outfit.Cynthia new Martron was looking at her thru his rear view mirror. She was a few years older than Tia an 18 year old senior in high school. She had beautiful hair that she despised versus India Remy weave. A light skin complexion, a lovely heart shaped face and a voluptuous shape she knew Martron would fuck her if he ever had the opportunity. Cynthia found him attractive, she was willing to give him a chance to have sex with her. Cynthia didn't speak, she waited for Tia to talk " Martron can we stay at the Marriott downtown please?" He quickly pulled his car down towards Albina Avenue heading south bond to downtown Portland. Martron had been to harsh to Cynthia. She didn't respond to his disrespect. Which made him feel like a bully. "Bitch sorry I jumped down your throat. Nyemiah was like A mom to me. What I don't want or need is no messy shit around me or my sister. Cynthia sat quietly texting on her phone. She would have usually, let him have it. Lethal or not no nigga ever disrespected her. The Beamer was parked by the Water Front Marriott valet, on the brisk spring evening. All three of the cars occupants entered the hotel lobby. Martron paid for two hotel rooms.

He asked for the hotel suites, one for himself and the other was for the girls. The suites were adjoined. They entered one of the hotel suites. Discussing everything but the death that had occurred . The rooms were plush ,with California king beds, flat screens televisions, patios with balconies overlooking all of downtown Portland it was a beautiful sight. Water Front park stretched thru downtown. The sky scrapers shined bright. Highlighted by the moon."Hey Martron do you got any Swishers? Nah but I got some tree." Cynthia questioned him. She chuckled while asking, for no apparent reason. "Nah I'm a go to the store. Yall can order whatever you guys want from room service. We good bro just get them Swishers." Tia wanted to smoke weed badly. She was not concerned with eating any food. Cynthia asked for Grey Goose and cranberry juice. The valet gave Martron his Beamer. He got Inside his car; listening to the new Trina cd. Tia loved the album; he started to cry. The hate he had for his father D-Loc ran thru his mind. He Merged into the downtown traffic as the sun completely set. Driving to the liquor store in the Pearl District he bought a half gallon of Grey goose Vodka. Leaving the liquor store he forgot the cranberry juice when his phone rang. "What the fuck you want Zayley are you coming back? where are you been ?

Martron Jr. miss you bitch you miss me! I just left

from y'all earlier and I always have our son. So cut

It out. Nyemiah is dead, who did it? nobody, she

overdosed, on what? I thought she only drank.

we all thought so. Man, Zayley my sister is waiting

for me at this hotel. You can bring her here baby.

Fuck no man I'm a hit your line later."Martron

hung up his phone and pulling into the Plaid

Pantry parking lot. He purchased cranberry juice,

a pack of Newport Short cigarettes and condoms he

hated Cynthia. He was still a man, she was

beautiful. Pussy was pussy, he couldn't wait to

have her screaming Piru. Martron returned to the

hotel. Taking the elevator to the 13th floor. He was

dazed from the weed he had smoked in his car, on his way back to the Marriott. He slide the room key in the card reader. A wave of sadness swept over his whole being. Tia was asleep, Cynthia was nowhere to be found. Suddenly he felt body heat behind him. Cynthia whispered in his ear.She had crept up out of the bathroom, approaching Martron. "I got in the shower cuz you was taking hella long," Her breast sat up nicely they were large and perky, her nipples sat hard, from the cool breeze. The hotels air conditioning affected her body temperature.Her shapely figure was barely covered by the small towel draped on her frame. It exposed her neatly shaved pussy. "Aye blood chill out with all of that cuz shit. I'm a crip bitch Martron that's how I talk Cuz! Whatever can I get some dome though? Yes let's go to the other room". Tia layed in the hotel bed playing possum, pretending to be asleep. She was wide awake as her best friend exited the room to go fuck her brother. She minded her business. Tia found the swisher sweets her brother had bought. She rolled a fat blunt just for herself. Walking into the porcelain covered bathroom. She smoked the strong weed with the shower on. Hot boxing the bathroom as she inhaled the entire blunt. Tia didn't partake in drinking but her mother had died. Leaving the bathroom. She poured herself two shots of the Grey Goose feeling the burning sensation of the liquor trickle down her throat. Tia wanted more. She poured two more shots,she went on drinking. "Yeah bitch suck that dick" Martron yelled at Cynthia. He slowly fucked her face speeding up his hip rotations every once in a while.He soon entered her cave. "Damn you crab bitches got some fire." Sweat trickled down his forehead. "Yes right there, baby right there, that's my spot! Martron stroked Cynthia from behind aggressively. The condom broke, he didn't stop sexing he kept going. She did not stop him from fucking her, she had never been fucked the way Martron was fucking her. He flipped her over, giving it to her raw,in the missionary position. He took all the frustrations out on Cynthias tight pussy. They climaxed together. He made it a point to pull out and release his cum all over her toned stomach. He was satisfied, she was as well they had both been extremely pleased. Feeling selfish he kneeled down consuming her pussy with his mouth like a predator attacking its prey. "Yes cuz, I will stop if you keep banging on me!" Cynthia quickly refocused and shut her mouth only letting out moans of pleasure. He ate her out for 30 minutes and fucked her in many positions until she climaxed four times.

Chapter 2

Tia awoke the bottle of Grey Goose lying next to her. She was still in the hotel bathroom. Her head spun she felt slimy, thick, vomit soak her face and hair. She had fallen asleep in a pile of throw up. She felt like the experience from the previous night was a big nightmare. Tia could still smell the crimson blood, that dropped from the syringe that killed her mother. Tia got up angrily throwing the empty bottle of liquor into the mirror shattering it. The mirror shattered into a thousand pieces.

Cynthia rushed into the bathroom "What's wrong best friend come here". Tia laid her head on her best friends shoulder. She wanted revenge. She knew she couldn't find any of the dealers that sold drugs to her mother because her mother kept her away from the streets.She wanted revenge on her father. Her mother had told her about the relationship with her father, Tia blamed D-Loc. Feeling as if her mother would had never been introduced to the street life if it wasn't for her father.The feeling was conflicting she loved her dad dearly yet held hate for him."Where's Martron Cynthia? He left to grab us some breakfast and some fits for the day." Tia rolled her eyes as her friend kneeled down to clean up the vomit. She asked Cynthia for some space. stripping naked, getting into the steaming hot shower. Crying as she bathed. Crying tears that she would never see her mother alive again.Her brother returned with food and clothing. Tia dressed in a crispy white tube top, red monkey jeans, clad in cherry red Air Force Ones. Cynthia was a talented braider. She did Tias hair in a neat side swoop of perfect cornrows. Tia had 85 missed phone calls from D-Loc and 50 missed calls from her boyfriend Kevin.

The only person that knew Tia was in a relationship was Cynthia. Kevin was square for the most part, a varsity basketball point guard attending Grant high school. He was 17 years old with aspiring dreams. He wanted to graduate high school and attend college for architecture. Kevin loved basketball and could easily be drafted into the NBA. He was just a young black man with different goals for his future. Kevin was light skin, with long flowing braids, his hair hung past his chest. He was mixed having a white mother and black father.He had a baby face perfectly placed dimples. Thick eyelashes on his doe like eyes. Handsome yet humble standing at 6'4 . The likelihood of Kevin growing taller was fairly high. He wasn't done growing, however he stood far beyond average height. Tia had met Kevin after one of the Jefferson vs. Grant basketball games. He approached her instantly attracted to her smooth chocolate skin tone. They exchanged numbers soon after they started dating. Kevin loved his girlfriends innocence. He adored her, loving how she kept her virginity. He was astonished that Tia was also well educated. They vibed on deep intellectual level.The only thing he Kevin didn't like about his girlfriend was her weed habit. He had tried weed when he was 12 years old never tried it again. He was a athlete and had goals that didn't involve getting high. Plus he didn't want to end up like any of his brothers.He was one of five boys his mother Samantha had given birth to.

Kevin's mother was a working class nurse at providence hospital. Kevin's mother was a square white women. It was his father who had led his other sons astray. Johnny Wayne was an original Hoover. Samantha knew from day one the gangster was trouble. Meeting him at a underground Portland State University party when she was attending the university. Samantha was a young women at the time coming from a prestigious family she was sheltered. Adoring black men, it was easy for her to in love with Johnny. He married her giving her five sons. That was about all he had ever done for her. He was a hustler he didn't work and didn't provide the money he made he kept for himself.Samantha was the sole provider for her family until she invested with her father into a car dealership. The business provided her husband with a career, making their family stable.Johnny was a bad influence,cussing , gambling, cheating openly ,raising his sons to his to be gang members. Kevin was different from his siblings. Loving school from kindergarten on up. His brothers Johnny Jr, David ,Mello, and Robert all made fun of him. Kevin was the middle son born after David which was his brother that he favored the most. Both Johnny Jr.and David had graduated from high school. That was a mandatory requirement to live in Samanthas home. Graduating was their only accomplishment gang banging and racking up babies mothers was their Forte'.Kevin only wanted one female and that young lady was Tia.

He heard the news of her mothers death it broke his heart. Kevin knew Tia had family issues not to the extent of what she was truly going through.The night of Nyemiahs death, Kevin sat in his bedroom idolizing photos of Tia on her a MySpace page. He had texted her several times and left her several messages in her inbox on her MySpace. Laying in his twin sized bed dressed down in a wife beater and Jordan basketball shorts. He stressed that he couldn't reach his girlfriend.They usually spoke all throughout the day. It was unusual for Tia not to respond to him. His brother Robert stammered in drunk. Clad in a Houston Astro's hat, orange flannel shirt with blue Levi's. He was sloppy drunk;claiming that Nyemiah was dead. There was major funk going on in the streets between the Hoover's and the Rolling 60 Crips. All of the drama was dangerous and deadly, any news of issues with the other side was enough to strike up conversation. Kevin sat inside his Buick century contemplating on how he would approach the love of his young life regarding her mothers death. All he could do was replay the conversation he had with his brother the previous night. "what's good square ass nigga probably online looking at the brand bitch, Robert watch your mouth Tia isn't a gang member, hood rat bitch, stop putting her in that category because of who her dad is. The nigga D-Loc still with the smoke anyways that's why you're really mad with your broke ass."

The brothers bursts out laughing loudly in their bedroom.The mood quickly turned somber. "Bro I heard some weird shit. What did you hear? Let me guess,David got another baby on the way by a raspy bitch? Nah bro it's serious man I heard Tias mother is dead ! stop playing? On Hoover I heard that. Man D-Loc gonna go nuts that was his babies' mama. We all know he loved that hoe groove."

Kevin shook his head at his brother. "Stop

disrespecting the dead! Don't speak on my girls

dead mama like that,what the fuck is wrong with

your drunk ass." Robert quickly cleaned what he

said up. " I wasn't saying it like that, we all know

Nyemiah was a hustler she got her doe.but what if

she was murdered ? I heard she was raped and

some more shit." Robert had misinformation like

most hood gossip. There was extra subject matter

added In and twisted stories. Kevin drove to

Woodlawn park to play basketball. He was in deep

thought on the early spring morning and needed

to release some stress. In need of a distraction

until he could figure out how to reach his girlfriend. He stood at the 3 point line shooting shots not missing the basket one time. Suddenly he was staring into the eyes of three Pirus. They were all friends of his girlfriends brother Martron. Madrix,Ronny ru, and Lamar, were known for killing niggas. Poping off on their enemies at any given time. They were all drug dealers and pimps. They loved pumping fear into their rivals. Lamar spoke, "Aye little snoove nigga what the fuck you doing here?"

Lamar was a huge nigga 6'2 weighing 290 all muscle. He immediately intimidated his peers due to his stature . He also was a skilled fighter and

precise with shooting he never missed a shot.
Kevin responded "I'm just hooping not grooving
all that banging shit corney to me". Kevin was a
square he was also known for being a skilled
fighter. He had hands taking his fare fade more
then once and winning. He wasn't moved by the
gang members.That still didn't mean he wanted
funk with them he just wasn't a coward. Kevin was
outnumbered, wishing his annoying brothers were
there to help him out in case shit got hectic. Ronny
Ru spoke up in Kevin's defense" Man Lamar leave
him a long," Ronny was a educated thug he took
his education just as serious as he took the streets
a student at Western Oregon University he came

home to Portland every other weekend. He saw a

lot of himself in Kevin following his stats, he had

personally been to a few of his basketball games.

Ronny sold drugs to pay for his college tuition. His

education was important to him. Ronny spoke to

Kevin. "Blood I know you not no snoove, but you

shouldn't hoop here no more shit brazy as fuck

right now bro." Although Kevin felt he could

protect himself If he fought the men one on one.

He was more then grateful that Ronny had given

him a pass. He quickly got inside of his Buick

pulling off, as tiny sprinkles of rain started to hit

his windshield.He drove in his own thoughts

Listening to LiL Wayne's "The Carter 2" album.

He sped to Cynthias house assuming she would know of Tias whereabouts.When he pulled up he noticed young niggas old on the block saling crack. He walked up to her front door and waited patiently.

Cynthias mother had met him before thru Tia she thought he was just an associate. She explained that Cynthia had left to stay the night with Tia and had notified her that they were at the Marriott hotel downtown.He thanked Cynthias mom and driving cautiously rain cascaded hard now. The weather frequently changed that way in Portland. He knew the room could not be in Tias name because she was indeed a minor, he thought it had to be in Cynthias name. The hotel clerk gave Kevin the run around, explaining she couldn't give information on what room a guest were staying in. Kevin pled with sincerity. The upcoming Monday would be the beginning of spring break. Both him and Tia had made plans to spend the vacation from school hanging out together. He daydreamed as the hotel clerk read him the policy rules. "Look I know that you guys aren't allowed to give out information. But my girls mother died last night. I need to see her, I was told that she is staying here." Suddenly the female clerk recognized Kevin. "Aren't you the point guard at Grant? My daughter goes there she is on the girls varsity team. Who is your daughter? Her name is Alison Wright. Oh Ally she is cool that's my classmate we have English together." The small talk led the clerk to give Kevin the Information he needed. The women was nosey ,paying close attention to what room guest occupied. Even the ones that were checked in when she wasn't on shift. As he reached Tias floor he became nervous wondering if she would even speak with him while dealing with grief. He thought to himself "Will my baby girl even talk to me". Once the elevator reached her floor he took a deep breath stepping off of it, on to the neatly cleaned hotel carpet. Cynthia opened the door with a shocked look on her face she began to stammer.

" Hey Kevin what's good? Is tia here with you? Is she okay ? Yes she is here hold up let me grab her." Martron heard the voice of a man at the door. He grabbed his glock approaching the door. Recognizing Kevin he knew he was well known in the basketball world. Martron also knew he was David's younger brother he didn't care for David one bit. He thought the nigga was a bitch and would funk with him on site anytime they ran into each other. He knew David was tough to stand up to deep down inside. Convincing himself that the young man wasn't a threat was crazy. Martron made himself believe David was a bitch. Kevin stood at the door, which made him curious , he kept his cool. "What are you doing here little nigga?" Tia crept up on the conversation in a daze she was out of it,not in a good state of mind. Kevin then said " I just want to talk to her that's all and I found out she was here and we are together". He spoke with his chest puffed up and out like he was a bad ass. Martron was impressed by Kevin's courage and demeanor.

He let him into the hotel suite. Kevin grabbed his girlfriend in an warm embrace hugging Tia. Explaining what he had heard; he wanted to be there for his girlfriend . Martron, Cynthia, Tia and and Kevin took seats in the suite. Cynthia on the couch ,Matron sat next to her, Kevin respectfully sat on a chair, while Tia stood. She explained what had taken place to everyone, going into detail regarding her mothers hidden addiction. There had been times she had to put her mother in a cold bath shaking her back to life. She cursed her father for being selfish and cursed her mother for the lifestyle she lived. Having a drug addicted, prostitute as a mother wasn't easy at all. Her mother hid her addiction well. Tia still was constantly embarrassed that her mother was a hooker. she could never say that her Nyemiah was

49

a good remodel or parent.She was selfish and had died on her.Tia looked at the others in the suite with tears streaming down her chocolate cheeks. Tia spoke sharply "She loved that dope more then me,I know she loved the streets and my dad more then me, but not no dumb ass heroine, she would get so strung out I believe she was even tricking for it a few times. My dad asked if she was on anything other then coke she lied,forcing me to keep her secret." She felt like she should had told her brother the truth he was her closest family member. Martron did not agree with her method of thinking. " Tia you did the right thing by keeping your mouth closed. Nyemiah was a proud women she would not had wanted people looking down on her." He looked at Kevin with a mean mug on his face. He talked in a rude, loud voice. "Lil nigga none of these words better ever be repeated. I'll kill you I swear on my kids." The two men began to exchange words. " I love Tia I would never do that, I ain't on no hoe shit don't make death threats though!" Martron couldn't believe Kevin had talked back to him. "Lil nigga I don't make threats". Martrons statement was known to be true. He was a killer, a hitter, a gangster that many men feared .Kevin knew not to get on his bad side. Martron observed the young man. Liking the way Kevin spoke to his sister. He wasn't ready to let her go however kids grew up much faster then they did when he was coming up.He was very happy that he was a square vs. a hood nigga.

   That afternoon as the four of them sat in the hotel suite. The Pathologists called with an autopsy report, reaching Martron. He wondered how the women on the other end of the phone had gotten his phone number?" Hello is Martron Brant available? Yes this is him speaking, may I ask who is calling me? I was calling in regards to Ms.Nyemiah Gibson." Martrons hand shook as he held the phone to his ear." He placed the phone on speaker. "Mr. Brandt ,Ms. Gibson died at approximately 9:45 pm March 15th 2005. She suffered from cardiac arrest." Martron was Confused by the doctors statement. "No disrespect but you're telling me she had a heart attack from a heroine overdose ? Mr. Brant that wasn't the only substance found in her system. Sulfuric acid which comes from a car battery was also found in her system. Those were the substances inside of her body which matched the substance inside of the syringe. Was there anything else in her system? No sir there was not. How did you get my number? We spoke to officers who said you were next to kin, to Ms. Gibson's teenage daughter." Rapping up the conversation Matron had been standing during the conversation he took a seat on the king sized bed. He only sat down for a moment. He leaped quickly, slamming Kevin with full force into the hotel wall. "Bitch ass snoove you came here to get in good and run back and tell your brothers the motherfucking business. You niggas think you're going to get away with killing my people huh ? this was some inside shit nigga I don't give a fuck what you say." Everyone was confused by the way Martron reacted to the phone call he was losing his mind. Tia stood up for her man. "Get the fuck off him he has nothing to do with what happened to my mother." Tia had never cursed at her brother he was saddened beyond hurt, he felt betrayed. "what the fuck Tia you must be dick whipped or something by this little nigga? you sound crazy ass fuck defending this sucka ass nigga. That's why you fuck with this punk ass crab bitch." Martron let go of Kevin he grabbed Cynthia by the throat. Yelling in her face " funky ass bitch I'll smoke you too,got my little sister fucking on this mark all y'all get the fuck out!" The three teenagers left the hotel driving back to the North East side of their city. The car was silent not even a peep of music played. They pulled up in front of Cynthias house. Grabbing her things looking up to the passenger seat at her best friend, Cynthia spoke. " I love you Tia, your brother loves you.

He's just mad speculating shit tripping. Call your dad you need to talk to him, go stay with him. If you don't want to you can always stay here my mama ain't running shit I love you bitch." Cynthia was a loyal friend she deeply loved Tia hating to see what she was going through. She wished she could cheer her up. Tia was somber she responded " I'm good Cyn thank you for staying the night and being here for me I'll call you about the funeral." Cynthia exited the car opening the passenger door she hugged her best friend hesitantly leaving. Kevin looked into his queens eyes seeing deep sorrow and pain. " Baby I'll be 18 in a month, I will get us a crib. I can get a place through my grandpa he owns property. I'm going to call my brother Johnny to get us a room for now." Tia had never stayed overnight with a boy. She was nervous, at the moment she needed Kevin more then she had ever needed him before. " please don't leave me Kevin. I won't Tia I love you baby girl" . The two kissed gently looking up In awe the young beauty was amazed as she wiped the moist tear floating down Kevin's face. He was crying for her. Kevin's older brother actually came to their rescue. Paying for a motel room for up to a full week.Once the two love birds were alone they laid next to each other staring into one another's eyes.The motel was run down, musty not what Tia was use to at all. Con webs sat in the side of the walls,the the paint was a dark yellow,the shag carpet was thin. Her whole entire life was changing, making her think she was ready for a big change sex.

" Kevin would you love me less if we did it? I'd love you the same we have been together for a year I wouldn't look at you any different then I ever have". He spoke honestly "Its a mature situation and I'd think your were a women making your own choices about your body and what you want to do with it. Would you think I was a hoe? I would never look at you as a hoe for making love to me or allowing me to make love to you." Kevin and Tia had spoke about her virginity often. He had sex with one other girl before their relationship. He was not experienced. Tia had planned to lose her virginity on her 16th birthday. At that very moment her emotions were taking over. She was heartbroken and vulnerable. Tia initiated the contact.Kissing Kevin slowly leading her tongue to his neck sucking it gently. They had kissed passionately. Tia had never sucked his neck.It made him nervous feeling the sensation of sexual power take over his body. " Tia are you sure you want to do this? I don't have any condoms on me cus I don't be fucking at all, Its okay baby I know you're good." Kevin was std free. Tia was young and naïve she didn't think about the ideal of pregnancy. Kevin then kissed her neck. He then undressed her and himself. Kissing her nipples, licking them In unison. He licked her belly button, placing his index finger on her untouched clitoris. He gave her head slowly taking his time. It was his first time performing oral sex.She moaned screaming "Kevin please don't hurt me." He placed his finger inside her box. She squealed in pain, telling him to continue. After four play for nearly a hour. He finally put the head of his 8 Inch penis Inside of her. He slowly popped her cherry, taking her virginity.Speaking the truth to her. "Tia I'll love you forever, I love you too Kevin."They made love throughout the night; falling asleep In each others arms.The couple didn't know they were staying at a motel that the Rolling 60 crips would frequent.They had been at the motel for three days.Coming from a dinner date at the Lloyd center Apple Bees Restaurant . Tia suddenly felt a nervous feeling.It was the same feeling she felt the night she found her mother dead. Kevin gave Tia the room key he was a gentle man locking the door to the car, then carrying their doggy bags.As he grabbed the bags happy in glee to be with his boo,gun shots began to ring out. He froze falling to the ground while his legs were on fire. He thought to himself " what the fuck is happening to me." Two gun men approached him clad In Seattle Mariners hats and jerseys. " Yeah David you ain't that hard now that your snoove ass got caught slipping". One of the young men said The other responded to his cohort. " Finish this nigga cuz". Four shots rang out shooting Kevin directly In his torso. Tia ran towards them as an onlooker tossed her to the ground shielding her frame. Tia saw them running away she knew the two young men . They were her fathers lil' homies Zoli Cuz and Tye. The gun men departed in a tricked out skraper. Tia ran towards her man. She had just witnessed the crips putting in work on Kevin, the results of mistaken identity.

" Baby please talk to me" Kevin didn't respond. Tia saw that he was still breathing. Her mother was dead , her brother hated her, and her boyfriend was dying in her arms. How could she prepare for her mothers funeral service with something so terrible happening to Kevin?

Chapter 3

The ambulance arrived quickly. The four of Kevin's brothers and his parents sat in the waiting room of Emanuel hospital, along with Tia. When the doctor walked towards the concerned family. The room became silent."Excuse me I need to speak with you all. Kevin was shot in his right calf, left thigh and four times in his chest. He successfully made it thru surgery. We removed all but one bullet in his chest. He will survive but he is very weak and unconscious in an Induced coma." The doctor that handled Kevin was a well known black provider. "I know you guys don't know me well. But your brother will most likely be in a wheel chair. He may be In one permanently. As a black man I really hope young black men can stop the black on black crime. Kevin will recover he may never be the same. But the cycle of violence has to stop. We all come from the same place. Our ancestors are rolling In their graves. It's not worth all the pain and suffering the community has to face. Please don't retaliate." The Doctor directed his comments towards Kevin's brothers; David shouted ." Nigga what the fuck you mean? My little brother almost died because niggas thought he was me. I'm fa sho' about to handle these niggas. Imma kill all the punk ass niggas. Fuck you're advice and fuck this punk ass hospital too." All the brothers agreed with David they wanted blood. Knowing the crips who had done the shooting weren't gangsters they could easily kill. Zoli Cuz and Tye were known for being hitters. Killing their enemies regularly. The family was not allowed to see Kevin, they were all disappointed.

Tia snuck past his room looking thru the window. Seeing Kevin hooked up to several machines quietly in his coma. Devastated the young girl, she did not want to be alone. Tia walked on the cold tile floors towards the lobby. Sucking up her pride, making a phone call to her c brother.

" Hello Matron, Tia where are you ? Are you all right? Tia I love you lil' sis and Im sorry. Im with Cynthia we gonna come swoop you where are you at?" Tia met her brother at Dawson park she didn't want him pulling Into the hospital parking lot. The last thing she wanted was more drama for Kevin's family. She knew her brother were his brothers enemies she made a wise choice. Martron got out of the car. "Tia come hug your dumb ass brother I'm so sorry, get in the car." Martron had heard on the street about the mistaken identity. Preaching to his little sister calmly. " Sis stay the fuck away from that David look alike ass nigga." Martron did feel bad that Kevin got shot because the young man was a square. Yet he cared more about his sisters safety. He didn't want her in danger from being around Kevin. She could had lost her life. " Tia look at me you're burying your mother tomorrow. I know you're in puppy love; but let's focus on Nyemiah for right now." Tia looked out of the window watching the rain drops drip down. Thinking how quickly her life had changed In one weeks time. She missed her mother while resenting her at the same time. Tia wished her mom never took the hot shot or any drugs for that matter. Tia had avoided an In depth interview with the police and she did not want to shame her mother and speak with them. Her heart was crushed, due to Kevin's condition. Assuming he would hate her because she was D-Loc's daughter. She knew he would feel like she set him up.

Martron attempted to pass a blunt to Tia, she refused it, just wanting to think with a clear head. It was 7pm the Lloyd center mall would close at

9pm. Martron drove to the shopping center so they could attain outfits for the funeral service. They all nodded their heads to the Ying Yang twins hit single " Wait". The song was a popular tune, they loved the raunchy lyrics ." Wait to you see my dick, aye bitch, wait to you see my dick, Imma beat that pussy up". Cynthia thought about a time her and Tia had enjoyed the song together. "Aye bitch remember when we first heard this at the party on 7th and Dekum a few months ago. Yes I remember that party was cracking. It was hella hot in there but it was fucking booming". Being in high school the girls went to a lot of parties on the weekends. Dancing the nights away. " Tia what do

you want to do for your Cday it's in two months?"
Cynthia asked with curiosity. She made sure to use
Crip terminology in front of Martron. Tia hadn't
even thought about plans for her birthday. Her
Sweet 16 was the last thing on her mind. All the
drama In her life she couldn't wrap her mind
around celebrating her birthday. She made up
ideas on the spot. " I don't know have a party or
throw a barbecue, it should be warm enough by
May".

   Once they arrived to mall, Tia wasn't excited
about getting an outfit to wear to the funeral
service. The day was stressful, they had to rush and
shop. Nyemiahs body viewing was scheduled for

8:30. They knew the shopping had to be done quickly. As Martron parked the Range Rover he drove, his instincts told him to take a weapon in the mall. He placed his 45. Caliber hand gun on the side of his hip under his white tall t-shirt. He left his other two guns under the car he never packed light having a 9mm and 357. Hand gun , As well. Placing those guns in his built in hiding spot under his back seat. The three stepped inside Meier Franks store signs showed the store would soon convert to a Macy's department store. The change would be different for Portland. Martron spoke to his sister " I know this store isn't really your style . Where do you wanna go? Wet Seal or

Rave is cool." Martron was disappointed In her response. " Fuck that cheap ass shit, sis at least go to Nordstrom's." He didn't want his sister to look tacky, being beyond materialistic he wanted her to wear the popular labels. " Sis how much money do you need? A good chunk of change if you want me to go to Nordstrom's. " Martron pealed off twenty one hundred dollar bills. Giving Tia one thousand dollars, giving Cynthia the same amount. " Aye Cyn don't get use to this type of treatment I'm only plugging you because you can't step in the funeral looking grimy . He chuckled lightly, knowing She had style. Heading to the men's department he yelled towards them "Don't but shit blue with my money either". Cynthia knew she would pocket her money she planned to steal her entire outfit, she was a well seasoned booster. Entering Nordstrom's the first thing that caught Tias eyes was a new coach purse, she didn't have it in her collection. However she wasn't there to shop for purses. Tia needed the proper outfit to represent her mother. She thought, " what would my mother wear?" Nyemiah always had a classy swag. That was difficult, for A 15 year old girl to capture. Cynthia had a better grown women sense of fashion. "What about this?" Cynthia held up a black BCBG silk blouse , with gold buttons down the middle and a black pencil skirt, with a simple cream stripe down down one side." Tia loved it the outfit screamed Nyemiah. " Let me try it on; Looking Into the mirror Tias green eyes watered. Her figure was identical to her mothers. She was becoming a women right before her own eyes. Seeing the change within herself without her mother In her life was a horrible feeling. Cynthia came to Tias' dressing room with her own outfit. Holding two pair of shoes for her best friend, to choose from. One was over the knee, leather,Steve Madden boots. The other was strapped, open toe Calvin Klein heels. Cynthia picked herself a black on black Guess pants suite, with black Swede open toed Guess pumps.In her arms she held the larger version of the coach purse Tia was eye balling. The purse was powder pink Cynthia grabbed the baby blue version of the handbag. She quickly removed each sensor off the items with her long fingernails. Tia whispered "Cyn what the fuck are you doing?" She was afraid. " Shut up getting our gear bitch". Cynthia placed the shoes and outfits inside the two coach purses. Placing both of the purses over her shoulder signaling her friend to follow her. " Come in bitch let's bounce." Tia was nervous not having one stolen item on her. She was still afraid to get caught. Once she saw Cynthia make it out the store she felt relieved. " Bitch you got balls, I never knew you was this cold with the boosting shit. I shoulda been coming to the mall with your ass. I told you before that I had skills Tia." Cynthia stuck her chest out like she was an Ol' G' She said a mini speech about her stealing abilities. The two girls were glad they got to pocket the money they were given for shopping. " let's go get our nails done." Tia loved having long claw like nails. "Cynthia call the weed man let's get a half I'm tryna get nooked." The two giggly girls headed to the nail shop located on the first floor of the mall. They were quickly serviced. The Asian owner knew they would be big spenders because of the coach bags they carried. The nail techs knew young girls loved expensive designs on their finger nails. Tia got a cheetah print design on her nails,while Cynthia

stuck to her flaming red nail color. She was a crip

but loved how the color red popes on her light

skin tone. While their nails were drying Martron

called Tias cell phone. " What's up bro, why

haven't you called me Tia, the crips is In here

thick come on , hurry your ass the fuck up." Tia

thought her brother was overreacting. Until her

and Cynthia stepped off the escalator on to the

second floor of the mall. She saw her brother

tussling with a known 60s crip Stacey. Martron

gave him combinations throwing the young man

off balance. Stacey wasn't a skilled fighter the

other men he was with looked like they were

going to attempt to jump into the fight. " Hell nah y'all niggas better not fucking touch my brother do you know who in the fuck our pops is stupid niggas". Tia screamed as she swung on the first young man that got to close to the fight. Tia knocked the shit out of the dude with her new stolen purse. Soon Cynthia was fighting another guy. The girls were losing but they didn't care. They couldn't stand back and watch Martron get jumped. Tia saw a gun out of her peripheral view. Martron pistol whipped Stacey holding him over the ledge.Staceys blood leaked down many feet to the ice skating ring. Mall security couldn't contain the small brawl. A store clerk yelled "look he's got a gun." Tia stopped mid swing "come on Martron we can't go to jail, fuck that Tia fuck any nigga that try's to test me on piru." He kept his grip on Stacey. Cynthia slapped Martron as hard as she could, bringing him to reality. "Come on now ain't the time or place they called the boys dummy." Martron quickly came to his senses the three of them scurried to the Range Rover. Martron chuckled as the merged on to the I84 freeway "Damn Sis y'all got major mittens. Cynthia you a rider for real for real. You shoulda been a blood baby." Tia was 140 pounds she held her own with the young men in the mall despite her weight. "Fuck we missed my weed man" Cynthia whined.

"Aye baby it's boo I got a ounce a nigga stay on with the tree." Tia just shook her head. Now her brother was referring to Cynthia as baby she had heard It all. He always made it out like he hated her friend. Tia thought his hate was so strong that he would kill her or put a hit out on her, his only intent was to murder the pussy. " We gotta hurry up we gonna be late but let's go to Madrix house to blow real quick. Cynthia don't tell nobody where my partna stay. I know you ain't no setup but don't fuck yourself over.

Madrix and Ronny Ru we're martrons best friends. He rarely saw Ronny because he was in college. Madrix on the other hand was his everyday nigga. Martron took the route of saling

dope mixed with money laundering. Madrix was a

certified pimp. When they were younger Martron

started saling 50 bubbles of crack. Madrix was a

player fucking all the neighborhood hood rats. At

16 years old he knocked his first hoe. His motto

from that day on was " put it in my pocket". They

pulled up to the 6 bedroom house in happy valley.

The pimp lived in a suburban community . At 26

years old he had managed his money right ,living

well. Martron owned the home his babies mother

Zayley lived in. At times their relationship was too

much drama for him to deal with. They also lived

in happy valley. He usually crashed at his trap

house in South East Portland. He knew it was time to purchase a home for him and Tia to live in. "What's up bro" Madrix said as he opened the front door to his house. Dressed in a Gucci silk button up shirt with Gucci silk pants. He was a pretty boy light skin, having long wavy hair, that he wore in braids or a slicked ponytail. He was 6'1 with an athletic build his most intriguing feature was his light grey eye color. Tia yearned for Madrixs attention. She knew she was to young, forbidden for thinking of him the way she did, she had a crush on him sense she was a young girl and that would not change. " I got tree let's smoke a blunt and catch up we running late to the funeral

home." Madrix spoke to Tia, "Come give me hug ,
aye wait Is this Cynthia the brand bitch?" He spoke
in a jokingly manner he knew the two girls were
as thick as thief's. " I fuck with your best friend
now nigga watch out,aye bro that's you?" Madrix
eyebrows raised. " Yeah that's me now nigga, are
you gonna move so we can come In and smoke."
Cynthias eyes grew large looking at the lavish life
Madrix lived. His foyer was decked out with a
small fountain, fish tank, rare plants and a large
crystal chandelier that hung over their heads. They
headed down the hardwood floor hallway to the
den. Cynthia was only getting a glimpse of the
décor as they walked down the long beautiful

hallway. The den was located in the back of Madrix crib. They sat on the burgundy sofas in the den. Cynthia Stared at the movie size television on mounted on the wall. Madrix turned on his stereo system dancing alone . To the late Mac Dres' "Feeling Myself". "I'm in the building and I'm feeling myself yadimeannn, feeling myself" Madrix sang alone he was in his own world. It wasn't rare for him to want to entertain guest. He turned to Cynthia who had saw staring with the sexiest look in his eyes. " You like what you see bitch? Oh no it's just that that your house is nice." Cynthia stuttered. " How you think I got this nice house? How you think I got this life?" Martrons nostrils flared Cynthia wasn't a hoe, Madrix thirsty antics rubbed him the wrong way. "Hold up baby I can see you me nigga is mad. Aye Mar Ru how many of your so-called girlfriends have I knocked? I think about 5 so chill the fuck out the bitch out there gang banging and sucking dick anyways. She need some motherfucking direction if you ask me." Martron was about to test Cynthia. "Nigga I ain't mad she's grown she can speak for herself. Cyn answer this dumb ass motherfucka!" Cynthia didn't hesitate. " I ain't gonna lie you live real nice. But so does my man and I ain't in to sucking and fucking to make no money, that ain't my style." Cynthia spoke with confidence. Tia just wanted her to shut the hell up. She wanted Madrix to go with his pimp rant she was amazed. He didn't rhyme or do all the punch lines he just talked she loved the way he finessed women. She saw what prostituting did to her mother she knew not to get involved with the lifestyle. Madrix babies mother Veda stepped into the den. She was young, 19 years old. Mixed with black and Asian, beautiful as can be. Standing at 5'6 her measurements were 36-28-40 she was snatched and thick. Her long curly hair hung to her ass she wore a green Versace dress, she had wedged Versace heels to match. She handed her babies father two thousand dollars. Returning home from hitting a lick. She was

Madrix bottom bitch, his main hoe out of the three women he had working for him. Veda was the only hoe that lived with him. She stuck her nose up towards Cynthia and Tia. Having young beautiful women in her house made her feel uneasy. She felt one of them,or maybe the both of them would step on her toes. "Bitch speak to my motherfucking company." Vedas eyes turned into slits. "Hi" she said dryly. "Get the fuck out my face go wash your stanking ass, then fix us some food you lazy ass bitch." Martron had to remind his friend that they had the viewing to go to. Tammy just pranced away not really giving a fuck what her manipulative pimp had to say. Martron shook his head at his friend, he disliked that he pushed the mother of his child to sale pussy.They had a son together Madrix jr. Martron thought of himself and how he never had a shot in life because of the lifestyle his parents picked. He could never see himself saling the mother of his children. Or any women he was involved in. He got his own money, He was not interested in pimping.

Tia ,Martron,Madrix and Cynthia all got into the Range Rover heading to the funeral home. They were high out of their minds. No one liked to deal with the trauma of death, not even the two killers In the car. They made it to the little chapel of chimes located across the street from Jefferson high school. They were In Rolling 60s'territory. Madrix had his guns ready just in case any funny shit happened to them . He was cautious because of the incident at the mall that his homie had filled him in about. Martron had gave Madrix a detail description of what occurred at the Lloyd center.

Before they could make it out the vehicle, gun shots rang out. Cynthia was Instantly shot in her right shoulder. Martron jumped out of the car, seeing the shooters were the same young men he had got into the altercation with at the mall. He shot stacey right between the eyes quickly. Taking cover Staceys homeboys weren't afraid they wouldn't back down Madrix had his friends back.

Shooting his pistol at the two other men. Tia found her brothers 9mm tucked under the drivers seat. She shot out the window in anger. Seeing her best friend lying there bleeding brought the beast out of her . She hit one of the Rolling 60s in the chest. They heard sirens. Leaving the area quickly they had to rush Cynthia to Emanuel hospital. As they drove Tia cursed " fuck no Cyn not you too". Her best friend was passed out she thought she was dying. Madrix yelled, " she In shook Tia she's not dying, remember when I took that slug to the chest last year the same shit happened to me." Tia listened to him, Madrix had nine lives he had been shot several times on different occasions so his words sounded like a doctors advice to her. When they arrived at the hospital Martron handed Tia his car keys fleeing in a cab . He knew he was hot from the scene at the mall he didn't want to be connected to the shooting. Cynthia was rushed In to have the bullet removed. Her mother stormed in angrily blaming Madrix. " So your gang banging, pimp ass got my daughter fucking shot? Bitch get the fuck out my face I don't even fuck with your daughter like that, I actually saved your brand ass daughters life bitch." Madrix disrespected Cynthias mother until he couldn't any more. " Ol Crab daughter having bitch. I'll blow your motherfucking brains out if you don't get out my face old ass bitch." Tia interjected . "It's not his fault she was shot by accident." Tia made up a story that they had arrived at the chapel. There was a random drive-by shooting which lead to Cynthia being shot. They soon wheeled Cynthia out she had suffered a flesh wound lucky to be alive that the shooting wasn't worst. " Cyn are you all right?" Tia exclaimed, "yes bitch I'm good blood." The chick that thought she was the hardest crip to ever breathe had transformed to the other side. The funk in Portland was surely heating up. The Rolling 60s Were not going to tuck their tails. Especially after they had lost one of their own.

They were just as viscous as the pirus and the

Hoover's , It was literally about to be

a body for body spring/summer.

Chapter 4

Meanwhile while D-Loc's Kids turned up in the

street. He sat in his beautiful mini mansion in the

Rocky Butte area preparing for the funeral.

Nyemiah was the only women he had ever some

type of love for in his life. He had beat her when

he was younger,not knowing how to control his

temper.As the years went by he grew up and out of

his abusive ways.He was a retired pimp. Tired of running and gunning.

The street life was all he knew for over 20 years. He wanted to settle down and have the family he dreamed of. D-Loc wanted to marry Nyemiah he loved her deeply, she had commitment issues. With what happened with her death it all made sense. The drugs was her husband. D-Loc had gotten the scoop on Nyemiahs death from his lil' homie Tye. He was upset that he had to hear the news in the streets before he heard it from his two children who ignored him. He wasn't the perfect father but he was always there for the two of them no matter the circumstances. He had been sitting in his tv room walking out of the French doors he decided to stroll down the foyer. Wearing the Tom Ford suit he would wear to the funeral service. He had it on for nearly two hours he couldn't take it off. He couldn't believe his boo was dead . The ringing of his cellphone took him out of his own thoughts . Seeing that his best friend of more then 20 years was calling he answered. " Whats up Stacey? What's up Is that my motherfucking son is dead cuz! He was shot outside your babies mamas viewing and they saying your son did it!" D-Loc was thrown off Stacey jr. was only 20 years old. He wasn't in the same age bracket as his son to beef with him. "That's a motherfucking lie cuz Martron

95

is a grown ass man what the fuck do he need to be in the mix with some young ass nigga like your son for." D-Loc wasn't sorry for Staceys lost he was aggravated that the nigga would talk to him over the phone about a murder vs. face to face. Especially accusing his son of murder. "Nigga it's not a lie your son did some foul shit so you need to tell his mama to get a black dress. Oh I forgot the bitch is dead , both your bottom bitches is dead." The 20 years friendship was out the window Stacey had started war. "Bitch ass nigga you better give your motherfucking mama the same advice and get the fuck off my phone with this hot ass shit. Nigga when you see me it's on sight no more words to be said." D-Loc hung up the call, Stacey had him fucked up to the tenth degree. Even if Martron was guilty of killing his son. Family came first. D-Loc spoke out loud to himself "Fuck! I gotta get in touch with Martron and Tia, goddamn kids." Tia was his princess his baby girl he loved her so much. Martron was his twin that he couldn't stand. He would ride or die for the both of them. He took off his designer suit. Changing into a black hoodie, black sweat pants, and black timberland boots. He was a Ol G', a skilled killer he had 12 bodies from Portland , to Arizona, California, Vegas and New York. He murdered most of the people in his home town. He wasn't proud of it, that didn't stop him from jumping back into the street shit in his 40s. He would take care of Stacey without creating beef with his whole hood. The Rolling 60s's were also family to him Stacey had just crossed the line.

Dloc got Into his Royal blue Bentley. With the biggest mean mug he could muster. As if his white neighbors were his enemies. D-Loc headed to Zayleys' house. Classic Tupac played thru his car speakers. " I ain't a killa but don't push me, revenge Is like the sweetest joy next to getting pussy." Both D-Loc and Nyemiah were fans of the late great Tupac. She had "only god can judge me" tattooed on her right thigh. Dloc had

"Ambitions of a Rider" tattooed on his back. He was beyond saddened and angry, he still drove the speed limit. He didn't want to bring heat to himself. He was armed, he also had guns in two tuck spots in his car. The guns would definitely get him caught up. D-Loc pulled into the gated community using the code 5500 that his son had gave him previously. D-Loc and Martron didn't keep in touch like a father and son should. The Happy Valley residence was the last known place his son had lived. Their relationship was strained, complicated to the max. D-Loc parked his car in the drive way that held a four car garage. The five bedroom home sat quietly. D-Loc didn't see any occupants scurrying around the home from the outside. He thought to himself " This little nigga think he somebody got a cool lil' spot built from the ground up. Lil nigga den stepped his game up." D-Loc rang the doorbell. Zayley yelled " who is this" in the valley girl tone she used when she spoke to strangers. " It's Darren". Zayley opened the door to her home. With two year old Martron Jr. on her heels. She had only met him a few times during the five year, on again,off again relationship She had with his son. They didn't know each other at all. Zayley wanted her son to know his grandfather. She choose to stay out of her babies fathers beef with his dad. She stayed in her lane when it came to the riff between the father and son. Martron resented his father, who was she to judge she had family issues like anyone else. " Darren hello come on in" D-Loc Stared at his grandson who was a spitting image of himself and his son. He then sized Zayley up she was 5'10, 180 pounds, a true stallion. Her figure was curvy in all the right places. She had a flawless skin tone, being Colombian and black she took good traits from both races. D-Locs' mind went back to his younger days. "Damn Martron wanna rip and run the streets, here his ass is sitting on a motherfucking gold mind. Zayley is a perfect example of a money maker." Viewing his sons babies mother like he viewed all women as a come up to make a profit. " Look Zayley I'm here because of Nyemiahs death. I need to speak to my son about some family issues." Zayley knew D-Loc was saling her drag, she could tell there was more to his story. He looked tense, stressed out, angry. She knew her place she wouldn't intrude. " Darren I'm so sorry I don't know what's up with him. He had only Called me once, since Nyemiahs death. We haven't even discussed myself and Martron Jr attending the funeral . I decided we are going anyways. I need to pay my respects." D-Loc saw the sincerity in Zayleys face. He was upset that he couldn't reach either one of his children. " I can't reach Tia either I've called her to many times to count." Zayley took a seat in her kitchen,trying to recall anywhere her babies father could be. " He is probably with Madrix , you know they rock tough." Thinking of his son hanging out with Madrix made his stomach turn. He hated the man Madrix had become, probably because he hated himself. "Well Zayley when you get in touch with him vice versus. Tell him I came here looking for him". D-Loc picked up his grandson giving him a loving hug and kiss before he left. Martron jr. didn't know his grandfather, however he still connected with him as if he had known him his entire life. D-Loc forced himself to leave if he stayed any longer. He would come out of retirement behind a women like Zayley, he was still a pimp at heart.

A unknown number appeared on Dlocs screen. "Yo who is this? Nigga this Johnny Wayne." Stacey,Dloc and Johnny had all grown up together. Although two of them were from Rolling 60's crip Johnny was indeed a Hoover. " This shit is getting to crazy out here in these streets. Man tell me about it. My son got shot the fuck up. Man I'm telling you this because I love you like a blood brother."

D-Loc listened seeing if he could still trust Johnny. He waited until he was silent to respond. " Whichh one of your sons got shot? Kevin!" Johnny response

was in a sad tone. " I talked to my son David,

word Is he was with your daughter, when he got

shot. I saw her at the hospital I didn't connect the

dots. I haven't saw her since she was a little girl."

Dloc was confused. " Why would my daughter be

around your son and why would she be around a

shooting?" Johnny wasn't going over specific

details he did let his friend know the two teens

were dating. " Tia is 15 years old she likes my son,

you know how these kids be. I was just calling you

to fill you in because your kids are in the mix just

like my kids are in the mix. Stacey called my

phone on some pick sides shit. The both of y'all my

day ones. That's fucked up lil Stacey gone. But these lil niggas don't be knowing the heat they getting themselves into." D-Loc blamed Martron although the shooting had nothing to do with Kevin . He would always blame anyone but himself for the destruction that was coming to Tia.

 Tia sat in a hotel room with Madrix. Her brother was laying low, Cynthias mother didn't want Tia at her house. Staying with Madrix was her only option. Due to the fact, that she would not reach out to her father. "Don't worry Tia Cynthia will be alright, it's just a flesh wound." Tia trusted Madrixs words. Since she had lost her virginity, she felt like she was a grown women. Tia Imagined

Madrixs' long tongue stroking her clitoris. " Tia snap out of it! Your brother told me to stay here with you tonight to make sure you was good. He's heading to Cali tomorrow after the funeral. He's giving me the doe to cop you a condo. I'll get you a spot near my crib so you can feel safe and loved at all times. If the spot I get you Isn't right by me. It will still be in a nice area, I'll check up on you everyday. You're going to live how you're use to living lil' sis. I promise you." Madrix words were pure, Tia was like a sister to him, she was innocent in his eyes.

" Madrix can you please stop calling me lil' sis Im not a kid. I'm fucking grown!" Madrix laughed at Tias' statement. " what makes you grown Tia? I get straight A's, I know how to drive but Martron won't buy me a car. And I keep my hair and nails done." Tia was naïve which caught Madrix attention. None of the things she listed made a women grown. Madrix had to check himself, he looked at Tia the wrong way for a few seconds. Forgetting she was his best friends 15 year old little sister. " Tia none of that shit make you grown. But what you got between them thighs can make you rich." Madrix didn't give a fuck quickly, he switched from big brother mode to pimp mode. " Tia is you a virgin? No I've had sex once." Madrix looked at her in shock. Most young girls he knew were full fledge freaks by her age. " Damn you

only fucked one time? yes only once! Tia take your

shirt off for me? Why are you asking me to take off

my shirt. I want to see what's under those fly

clothes you be wearing? Your pretty ass always got

on nice shit , I just wanna see what's underneath."

Tia thought "should I really show this nigga my

tities?" He caught her off guard in mid thought

planting kisses on her neck. Holding her close

letting her know he was not going to stop even if

she asked him to. Tia could feel his 10 inch dick

harden in his pants, she didn't relent. Madrix

kissed her on the lips roughly. Sending chills

down her body. He was grown with what he did to

her the experience was far different from what she felt with Kevin. He eased off all of her clothes, softly pulling her hair. Sucking on her collar bone. He licked her perky tities with excitement. He kept his game face on. He was known for piping any female down. He was fully dressed displaying all his attention to Tia's body. He licked and sucked on her belly button. Sliding his pointer finger down her clit, then in and out of her warm cave. Her body craved him. She was in love, he was in deep lust. He stopped leaving Tia lost. " Once we fuck you're mines. You understand that right? Yes I do ! I don't do love, I don't do one bitch . Can you handle that? Yes I can! Tia had so many thoughts in her head, the number one thought was she had always loved Madrix. She also thought the whole situation was wrong. Tia was only caught up in a dilemma, for a spilt second. Before she could refocus. Madrix grabbed his keys. " Tia I don't feel comfortable with this I'm going to get my own room." Tia jumped up from her position on the bed. "No it's not wrong please don't go, I'll do what you say." Madrix knew he had her right where he wanted her. He had quickly manipulated her mind by pump faking her like he was going to leave. Madrix kneeled down eating her pussy with passion. He wanted to give her the best sex of her life. He wanted her under his spell. Madrix ate her pussy and ass, introducing her to freaky grown sex. Tia squealed moaning his name the entire encounter. They had sex in every position Madrix could muster up that night. He even slid inside Tias back door. The two woke up to a phone call from Martron to be at the church early. "Look Tia don't tell your brother shit , he will never understand us. Its good your brother leaving to Cali. We can really do our thang."

Tia knew Martron would kill Madrix, if he ever found out they were romantically involved. She was a teenage girl, he was a grown man. The situation in itself was wrong. Madrix sexed her once more whispering lies,hopes and dreams. The two dressed heading to the church for the service. Stepping into the sanctuary felt like The source awards In the 90s. Nyemiah had a lot of so-called friends. Showing up becausee they wanted to be seen. Martron rushed to his little sister kissing her on the cheek. He greeted his best friend, not knowing that he was a snake. Both Tia and Martron departed from the sanctuary Heading to the basement of the church. Where the few members of their family were. D-Loc approached his children. "What's up Martron , hey Tia give your daddy some suga babygirl." Tia hesitantly gave her father a forehead kiss and a hug. D-Loc told Martron he had been looking for him at

113

Zayleys home. Martron whispered to his father. "
Yeah nigga I know you went to her house stay the
fuck away from her, stay away from my son and
stay away from Tia." As his words left his mouth; a
church usher announced , it was time for the
family to be escorted into the sanctuary. Tia cried
the entire service. When she viewed her mothers
body she almost fainted. Her mother looked
beautiful in a cream Armani paints suit. Her
favorite diamond necklace from Tiffany's and co.
sat in her neck. She looked like a run way model
taking a nap. A lot of people Tia barley knew
spoke during the reflections portion of the service.
Mostly ex hoes, and local fake people. Whom never

cared about Nyemiah when she was alive. At the
cemetery Dloc approached Tia and Martron.They
stood in a crowd with Madrix Ronny Ru along with
some of the other L.O.0 and Woodlawn park
bloods. Dloc just wanted to be in his kids presence
he spoke in a inviting tone. " Hey y'all I'm
throwing a little repast kick back at my place.
Y'all more then welcome to come." He spoke to his
kids in unison Martron knew his dad was inviting
the both of his children. He attacked him about
speaking to his own daughter. " Nigga get the fuck
out my sister face. You crab ass nigga." Martron
had disrespected his father in front of the large
crowd of people that had attended the funeral.

D-Loc was not shy to confrontation. " Watch your mouth you slob ass nigga I brought your ungrateful ass in this world, I will take you the fuck out!" The crowd all stood back watching the argument as if it Was a mini soap opera. " Well take me out you old ass nigga I'm not fucking scared of you blood." Martron swung on his father, The hit didn't faze D-Loc. He used his weight against his son forcing his back against a near by tree with a shove. With one hit to the jaw he sent his son to the ground. D-Loc was still a skilled fighter. He was still the parent,his son would never be able to beat him in a physical battle was what he thought. D-Loc headed towards his Bentley he yelled.

" Tia call me when you stop fucking dat disrespectful, slob ass , son of mines." Martron got up from the ground coming to his senses. He ran towards his father yelling back " Nigga what did you just say about me? I want my motherfucking daughter to be saved from this street shit and she won't be around your dumb ass. Let her live her damn life. If you want some funk With me so be it! Tia if you need to come stay with me I'm still your father. You're always welcomed." Tia stood silently. She had never lived with her father, he hadn't been the ideal father. Martron was disgusted . " You not her father you punk ass nigga! My sister is well taken care of." D-Loc got into his car shutting the door loudly, pulling off. He wouldn't tell his prideful son. That he planned on bodying Stacey and whoever else came against his him. Martron was angry he punched the window to his Beamer shattering it. He was losing his head, everything was happening to fast he gave out instructions preparing to leave to California. " Madrix make sure Tias spot is taken care of, Zayley keep you're ass in the house don't go no where right now niggas on my head,Cynthia take care of that wound lil homie." Cynthia didn't say anything she knew Martron was in front of his babies mom. He had to play the role of them being only friends. She knew the rules of being a side bitch. " Im going out there for a month to two months till shit die down out here. Tia your going to stay out here until the end of the school year. Then I'm buying a house in Arizona we need a fresh start." Martron handed Madrix an envelope with 25 thousand dollars in it. " Make sure you lease Tia a spot and keep her tucked away there until I get back school and home that's it." Before Martron could finish his sentence shots rang out. He saw David smirk out the side of a blue Hummer truck, as he shot several rounds from a A.R 15 gun. Martron couldn't help but to think of his young son

119

being there. He covered Martron jr. and Zayley using his body as a shield. Ronny Ru was shot eight times. Once the Hummer speed thru the rocky road Of Rose city cemetery. Martron, Madrix and Tia all ran up to Ronny who was gargling on his own blood. It was a horrific sight. They were all sad watching him die. Ronny had a bright future he was one of the young gang members that had made It out the hood. Martron vowed to kill every one of the Hoover's to avenge his homeboys death. He knew It would be war the Hoover criminals were treacherous. Their gangs body count was extremely high. They were the most hated hood in Portland. " Tia go with Madrix I

wanna kill at least 100 Hoover's before I leave."
Martron didn't wait for the ambulance to arrive.
He left seeking revenge. Tia sat in the hotel room
with Madrix replaying the horrible day in her
head. Her fathers words repeated like they were
tape recorded.She was afraid her life would end
behind her brothers street life.However Martron
had nothing to do with Ronnys death. David knew
the time and place of the funeral and burial. He
wanted To kill Tia. He felt she had set his brother
up to be shot. In his mind she was a Crip bitch. Her
father being a Ol G' didn't help her credibility.
Kevin would be leaving the hospital, within two
days. He had been taken out of the induced coma.

He would have to learn to walk again, he needed physical rehab.

David sat by his bedside hurt; he felt Kevin was the only one of his siblings that would amount to anything.Kevin slept peacefully,David wanted to wake his brother and tell him his new strategy for killing Tia.He planned on kidnapping Cynthia to lure Tia to him. He removed his Houston Astros hat placing it on the knee of his holester jeans. He felt no remorse for Ronnys death. He was a brand, he wasn't one of his niggas so why should he care was what he thought.Kevin woke up groggy.

"What's good bro?"Kevin weakly spoke. "Nothing lil' nigga. Just glad you okay is all I think about when I come up here. Stop being extra I'm a soldier, while you dummy's out there funking ready to die I'm living." David was not intrigued by his brothers words. " Look nigga I got at that bitch today. You did what? Nigga don't play stupid why do you think you here groove? The bitch clearly set ya ass up. No she didn't!" Kevin was angry that his brother would accuse Tia of doing something that would bring harm to him. " You mean to tell me the shit that happened to you was a fucking accident. Well word got back to me I got that nigga Ronny Ru". Kevin was hurt he liked Ronny, he remembered him giving him a pass. "David you're wrong for that. If you was after Tia

123

you fucked up anyways getting the wrong target.I don't give a fuck about that nigga.

You shouldn't either.Them niggas are against your flesh and blood you sound stupid on Hoover you sound dumb."Kevin layed in the hospital bed irate. He couldn't justify killing no matter who it was. Resenting black on black crime.

Chapter 5

3 months later……..Tia stood in the bathroom mirror checking herself out. Her hair was In a weave,jet black 18 inches long, In a neat center part. It flowed down her naked back as she applied her makeup she picked out the colors. Emerald green eyeshadow, a rose red blush and

nude lipstick to finish her look. Stepping into her beautiful bedroom she grabbed the money green Fendi dress. From her closet sliding it on. The dress covered only a small portion of her chocolate frame. Madrix walked up behind her placing a silver Tierra on her head. " Happy bday love, you look sexy ass fuck good enough to eat. Come here and sit on daddy's lap. It was Tias Sweet 16. Madrix had went all out . Renting out the underage Barracuda club In downtown Portland. He wanted to show her a good time, she was his prospect after all. Tia was excited; In three months time she felt she had grown up so much. She was living In a plush condo. In the Pearl District, a up and coming area In downtown Portland. She had a red Lexus sports car , which Madrix convinced her he bought. Knowing It was her brothers money that purchased it. Tia had dropped out of school taking Madrix advice. He had told her " You need to spend more time with me education is important. But what we have is more important."

He wanted to be as close to her as possible to fully manipulate and control her. Tia obtained her G.E.D the next week. Her living situation was what rebellious teenagers craved . No rules making her feel like a grown up. She walked into the kitchen seeing an unopened letter from Cynthia. She took the time to read It.

"Dear Tia

Hey boo I know your birthday is coming up. I miss you so much please go by and see my mom. Please come see me, I'm so lonely. I wasn't going to take a deal but I am. 18 months ain't that bad. I never thought I would be in this predicament. Imma finish my diploma though.Ive been on the phone with your brother a lot. He seems okay but I know he wishes he could come back sooner he misses you so much so do I. He has my books on stack mode so don't trip. Imma close this letter tho with love. Happy 16th birthday bitch.

Love Cyn real bitches do real thangs."

Tia looked at the pretty, pink birthday card chocking up. The inside read " Happy birthday bitch,sorry I'm not there but get hyphy for me."
 Cynthias letter and card were meaningful to Tia. She thought of her best friend often. A day after her mother's funeral, Martron was on the hunt to kill. Cynthia was right by his side. She wanted to be his rider die bitch. They sat in his Range Rover on a cool night, taking a break from the madness he had planned. Indulging in a session of weed smoking. They sat in the back streets of north portland, getting high. After they were done smoking they pulled into traffic on Interstate Street. Where the flashing red and blue lights

lurked behind them. It wasn't uncommon for a young black man, in a European car to get pulled over.

The officer searched the car saying he had probable cause. Martron's expired tags were his excuse. Upon the search he found Martrons 45. Caliber hand gun. He didn't have time to place the pistol in the tuck spot. Both Cynthia and Martron were taken into custody. When questioned they both stayed silent. Martron used his phone call to contact his lawyer. He didn't need his Lawyer Cynthia claimed the gun. Believing that since she didn't have any prior criminal history, she would be set free. Instead Cynthia was used as an example. The District Attorney wasn't giving her a break. He wanted young girls to stop taking gun charges for gang members.

Tia whipped the tears away before her makeup was destroyed. She heard Madrix humming in the bathroom she didn't want to ruin the night he had planned for her. She sat down on her comfortable California king bed deciding to go to the balcony to get some fresh air. She was dressed all except her Emerald green Gucci pumps. She dismissed putting them on. Placing her pedicured feet on the cool concrete of the balcony.Tia felt she had nobody but Madrix. That was the way he wanted her to feel isolated, that way he could have complete mind control. Martron left Portland soon after Cynthia went to jail. He knew he was hot, he stuck to his plans to go to California. He had a Inside scope on what could come his way. He paid a dirty federal agent. Giving the agent three kilos of pure cocaine monthly. He updated Martron that he had to be careful. The feds were watching him due to the recent way he conducted himself in the streets. Martron planned to return to Portland when the drug indictments on the other big time dealers ceased. Niggas were getting knocked left and right. He didn't want to be one of them. He stayed in contact with Tia,Madrix, Zayley and Cynthia.

Missing his little sister dearly believing she was in good hands with his closet friend.

Tia gazed at the stars happy and sad all at the same time. She missed Cynthia, she really missed her brother she even missed Kelvin. Madrix had made her delete Kevin off of MySpace. He had no way to reach out to her as he recovered. She was to afraid to reach out to him. Madrix also forced her to change her phone number. Relocating to the condo only made matters worst for Kevin to find her. Cynthia was the last link to her. She sat in the county jail preparing to go to prison. Kevin gave up. Madrix crept up behind her " Tia ain't you gonna put your heels on? I paid enough for them motherfuckas." Madrix laughed at his corney conversation. "I was just out here thinking. I got a letter and card from Cyn today. I also spoke to my brother this morning." Madrix felt as if Tia was holding back. "You mean to tell me you out here sad after all I've done for you? Look bitch if you sad over that snoove nigga just go back to that nigga then. I'm not sad over no nigga, I never said that, Tia I know you ain't getting loud with me. Bitch since you grown enough to get loud suck my dick right now on this balcony." This wasn't Madrix first time raging out on Tia. Madrix had to calm himself down. He didn't want to run her off before he completed his mission to fully turn her out. Her 16th birthday was the moment he had been waiting for. He was a pimp a strategic one. He had hoes including his babies mother. Veda was the H.B.I.C., wifey the bottom bitch. Veda had gotten beside herself.she wanted a family she constantly was trying to play house with their son. Madrix wasn't having it he wanted her to remember she was his hoe that's what she would always be.He had talked her into keeping the child. He looked at his own son as a money bag. Knowing that with an extra mouth to feed Veda would have to hoe harder. He didn't respect her, he allowed her to share her body with strangers to benefit from It. Had he loved her he wouldn't share her with any one, nor put her in situations where she could lose her life.

Madrix planned to mold Tia into the ideal bottom bitch. He wanted her to take Vedas spot. He would send her across country. He wanted her to touch the beasty east coast, Midwest and the south. She couldn't just be a west coast hoe. He wanted to test Tias loyalty the most; he knew she would make a killing. Tias beautiful face, her curves, and her book smarts would make him millions. She was the fantasy every old trick desired. The entire package. Her looks were rare the chocolate skin with no blemishes plus the green eyes she had would entice anyone. Madrix saw a high profit margin in Tia. Her pussy was tight she was young and naïve it was going to be a easy way to make more money. Deep in his come up thoughts. Madrix snapped out of the trance, back into the man with the plan for a lovely Sweet 16. "Tia Im sorry, I just get in my head when I think you on that nigga Kevin that's all.That's not the case Madrix sometimes I just wonder what we are doing? You got me living all nice. But you make it clear that we are not a couple.You leave me here alone a-lot and you flip out over the smallest shit, and now you're throwing me a big function it's confusing." He wanted her confused, she felt like she had somewhat mastered his mood swings. Tia wasn't even close. " Look Tia I get money and I never hid that,I'm a pimp baby so sometimes I talk crazy, but I'm still throwing you a Sweet 16. I feel bad with all that you have been thru." Madrix exclaimed as he stroked Tias cheek, he kissed her softly. "Tia look at how fly ya nigga got for you! Imma be the cleanest nigga in the town tonight.you the flyest bitch so why are you bugging?" Tia couldn't deny how good Madrix looked rocking a green Milwaukee fitted cap, green and white Rockawear button up shirt,blue denim holster jeans topping his outfit off with green and white nike air Jordan 1s'. Madrix diamond grill shined in his mouth. His diamond cross chain hung down to his dick he purposely did that. Mimicking the popular Gucci Mane song "So Icy." Tia looked at Madrix regretting ever being mad at him. She thought he was the flyest man breathing.

The two took two blue dolphin ecstasy pills. Madrix loved the drug, he had introduced Tia to the substance. He enjoyed weed and cocaine as well he didn't drink much. Vibing more off party drugs.Turning Tia out to taking thizz was easy after her mother passed. The little pills made all her worries go away, they made her feel alive, reborn. Madrix snorted three neat lines of cocaine off the marble tv stand in the bedroom.While Tia drank four shots of grey goose upping her buzz. The two headed out in Madrixs' red Escalade truck. Enjoying 50 cents hit song " In the club". It was for sure Tias birthday, the two would pull up to the club as ghetto royalty.Madrix had the club entrance draped out with red carpet. Chocolate fondues in the inside, ice sculptures and several poster size professional photos of Tia.

Madrix handed his keys to the valet. Escorting Tia In by the arm. He went against his pimp code of having her walk behind him with her head held down. He was a nigga with strategy so it didn't matter. Tias eyes gawked at how many people showed up to celebrate her birthday with her.

There were 100s' of people in the two story club partying.

People were walking up screaming happy birthday to Tia. Shaking Madrix hand.Some of Martrons other friends were clearly drunk. Looking at Tia like she was a good Item they could consume. "Damn Tia you look good, damn Tia you wearing that dress, wow Tia you're fine as fuck." They were giving compliments they wouldn't act on. Nobody knew what Madrix had going on with Tia. He would be murdered if anyone knew the truth.

All of the L.O.P's thought Madrix was being a good friend to Martron looking after his younger sister.Tia moved to the dance floor with Madrix on her heels. They danced with space in between them.Madrix wouldn't publicly grind on Tia he didn't want problems with Martron, nor did he want problems with any of his other partners. Madrix whispered in Tias ear. "I'll be right back baby". He had spotted a young while female dancing like a stripper on the dance floor.

Tia saw him approach the women, she didn't care she was high out of her mind.She swung her hips to the beat of David Banners song "Play" she felt someone grinding on her from behind. Perplexed because she knew Madrix wouldn't do such a thing in public. She turned around finding Kevin behind her. " Happy birthday Tia! Kevin why are you here?" The two yelled over the music. "Come over here by the bathroom where we can hear each other better." Kevin was letting Tia know he was going to get a conversation out of her.Tia didn't want to deny her first true love. Kevin looked and smelled amazing. He had cut his braids off rocking a philly fade. His mouth shined with a platinum grill. He wore a burgundy and white Abercrombie and Fitch sweat suit with white Air Force ones.Tia walked to the bathroom area with Kevin,keeping a lookout for Madrix. "Kevin this is not the time or place to discuss the past, let the past be the past. For real Tia you can't be serious? I've been looking around for you're ass for the last three

motherfucking months."

  Tia was surprised by Kevin's tone with her. She

immediately thought the shooting had turned

Kevin into a thug.She was far from right. " Nigga I

know your bitch ass didn't roll up in here to my

function getting smart, Tia for real now I'm a

bitch? I'm a man and Ive always had your back. I

went up to Jeff looking for you.I found out you

dropped out of school. I couldn't find you no

where so yes I came to your party to drop of a gift

for you. Tia turned around looking for Madrix

upset to see Kevin had came to her party with his

brother Johnny. None of the bloods tripped out on

Johnny. They respected him when Martron departed he started negotiating deals with other gang members regarding saling his product. Martron eventually gave his distributors permission to work with Johnny. Indeed he was David's brother. However He was also a hustler who would go hard and get it out the mud. Johnny had grown tired of banging just to bang he had turned into a true hustler.

Tia dismissed Kevin even more. "Nigga Im grown you really on some burnt out ,messy ass, shit! Plus why in the fuck is your brand ass here in the first place. Now Im a brand Tia? Cut It out you ain't built like that! Don't come at me with a attitude because I'm in a good position In life and my brothers eating too. I never knew you were a hater." Tia was upset that Kevin had came back at her with the truth. Everyone knew The Hoover's were starting to get major money. The hood that was the most hated was usually the one the females flocked to the most. Tia had never considered herself a gang member before. She had become a groupie for the bloods due to her secret dealings with Madrix. Dumbfounded as Kevin continued to rant. " I'm not that same little ass boy you left in the hospital bed I'm a man now. At one point I thought I'd never walk again. Look at me now Im still motivated, looking and feeling great so you can't tell me what function I belong at. All I wanted to do was wish you a happy birthday. But guess what bitch fuck you!! Fuck this gift." Kevin took out a rectangular jewelry box throwing it continuing to curse her out. " And if any of you other broads are listening. I don't fuck with raspy ass, wanna be gang member ass bitches. By the way I got accepted into Georgia Tech."

Kevin stormed off bumping into Madrix near the juice bar area. Madrix had to double take to make sure Kevin wasn't David. He still did not care for Kevin. He cold clocked the young elite gentleman in his face. He stumbled Johnny Jr. came to his brothers rescue. He knew his brother could hold his own. But family always came first. Johnny was on his business tip he allowed Kevin to strike Madrix back he then broke up the fight. Family was important , however he couldn't provide for his family if he didn't have the funds to do so. Jumping Madrix would cut him off with Martron he could not afford that. Kevin drew out a 357. magnum hand gun. Pointing at Madrix who was surprisingly unarmed. He was a man who always used strategy. Quickly played the cool role with Kevin. "Aye lil night I don't want no problems, well watch who you swing on then, if we didn't have a audience I would pop you're ass. Niggas get the game fucked up thinking just because I'm not a gang member I'm a weak nigga. Never that!"

Kevin then punched Madrix with his empty hand

dropping him to the floor. " Now that's what I call

a dirt nap ladies and gentlemen."

 No one knew how Kevin got the weapon inside the

club he kept it pointed at the crowd walking out

the door. The bloods tried to follow him. Kevin

had fully recovered from the shooting. His legs

were back to moving properly. Once he was out

the door he ran to the car at full speed.

 Tia had missed the whole fight she was freshening

up after her and Kevin's spat. Madrix burst into the

bathroom angrily. Snatching Tia by her arm.

"Parties over everybody get the fuck out." Madrix

screamed to the random women in the restroom. Tia knew the scene he was making was the quiet before the storm. The two quickly exited the club, exchanging no words. As they headed down the I5 freeway it took Tia a while to notice they were leaving Oregon. " Umm Madrix where are we going? You wanna know don't you Tia? Yes can I know?" Madrix wanted to beat the shit out of Tia. It wasn't the way he operated so he stayed In his Pimp mode. "Tia I've been looking out for you now it's time you look out for me. I planned this for tomorrow but your boy Kevin trying me at your party sped shit up." Tia was confused not knowing her ex and new lover had gotten into a fight. " I planned for us to pack take a flight first class all luxurious and shit. But your little snoove boyfriend ruined that. So we are driving. Where are we driving to? Where are you taking me!" Tia yelled at the top of her lungs. We are going to Vegas you're about to do some high class hoeing.

Tia was shocked. Madrix job was to look out for her not pimp her out. " Nigga imma call my brother! What are you gonna tell him? That you do drugs, you dropped out of school, that you been fucking and sucking me to have nice shit." He played mind games well. Her brother had made sure she would be comfortable and stable not Madrix. "Why not get paid for it slut ass bitch! You been taking dick in the mouth, pussy and ass

bitch!" Madrix had even Introduced her to

threesomes which made her uncomfortable.

Participating because she loved him. " Madrix I

really don't want to end up like my mom. You

won't, conversation rules the nation. You know Im

not a motherfucka that's prone to using riddles.

But if you got enough game you will barley have

to fuck. You're beautiful you will do just fine.Aint

shit wrong with hoeing , bitches get it twisted

fucking for free and shit. You're smart right? Yes

Im very smart. Well then why sale yourself short

then."Tia had barley turned 16 years old she was

overwhelmed. She wasn't a prostitute yet she was

in love with a pimp. There was no logic behind her feelings. Tia had never planned on being a hoe, but Madrixs' words were misleading.

D-Loc sat in his bedroom bored watching television. He pulled out his phone sending a text message to Aujanique. She was a female he chopped it up with from time to time. They texted back and forth for a few minutes. He then felt the urge to call her. "Can I take you out to dinner Carmel queen? Yes I would like to go out to dinner with you. How about I take you to Portland City Grill? That would be wonderful." D-Loc had met Aujanique a month prior.She came over to his place quite often. They had met at The Clackamas

Town Center Mall. He saw the caramel complexed women strutting in the food court with her two twins sons. Aujanique was a caregiver at an adult foster home. She made okay money. D-Loc helped her out a lot, although he barley knew her. He admired he work ethic , he admired that she was a devoted single mother. D-Loc had never respected women. Nyemiahs death caused him to turn a new leaf. He wanted to settle down and lead a square life. Aujanique was the perfect match. D-Loc was twelve years older then her. She wasn't into dating much,he had intrigued her. The two hadn't had sex which Irked D-Loc. He would be patient, he had to be in order to date a women of her caliber.

The very next day D-Loc headed to Aujanique's home to pick her up for their date. He played Jodeci "Stay" as he headed to her home. The song was setting the move for the evening he had planned. He wanted her to feel like a queen. He feigned laying the pipe down on her by the end of the night.

Aujanique sped around her house, her teenage sister who also lived with her sat annoyed with her arms crossed. " Sis why do I have to watch them I wanted to go downtown to this party.Tiffany your 15 years old you have no business at all these parties you go to. I wish I never had to live with your stuck up as, you're a stuck up bitch. Tiffany watch your motherfucking mouth before I have to get ghetto up in here.Your little fast ass is spoiled rotten. You don't need to go out every weekend. I work my ass off to take care of you and the boys one night can't be that serious. I like Darren and I may be staying overnight with him so deal with it. Wow Aujanique you finna get some dick? Watch your mouth little girl. Yes I want to sleep with Darren I'm a grown women and I like him. You just worry about keeping your virginity on lock from them hungry niggas." Tiffany was beautiful and thick,a red bone stacked in all the right places. She had thick reddish hair and freckles with beautiful black girl features. Large lips, a broad nose and beautiful large eyes. Aujanique worried about her little sister. She had been fast in the pants at a young age. Her 13 year old sons were the proof.Having them at 16 made her grow up fast. Her mother and father died in a car accident two years prior leaving Aujanique as the guardian of her younger sister. "You do look cute sis. Thank you Tiffany." Aujanique had on a white Gucci blouse D-Loc had bought her denim seven jeans with white Gucci pumps he also purchased. Her long Indian Remy weave hung flowed down her back. The two sisters talked and laughed until they heard the doorbell ring. "Tiffany can you go get that while I put the finishing touches on my makeup." Tiffany opened the door. " Hey Darren, Hey Tiffany how are you? I'm good, please treat my sister nice. I will you don't have to worry." In the middle of their conversation D-Locs phone rang the caller I.D read unknown. " Hello who Is this? Pops? Hey Martron how are you? I'm good dad." The two hadn't spoken since the fight at Nyemiahs funeral. " Pops have you heard from Tia? I talked to her briefly on her birthday. I bought her a purple Beamer sitting on 22's, that's nice of you pops. I sho' did but she hasn't met up with me. Son can I ask you why you have her staying with Madrix? Why not that's my best friend? I understand he's your partner but Madrix is a pimp. He's a pimp first before he's your friend son trust me. He would never come at Tia like that blood. You know how slobs move anyways son y'all niggas weird anyways.That's your opinion dad." Dloc laughed out loud from gang banging on his son. He shifted back to serious mode. " I would hope not for his sake. On Rolling 60 crip he will be a dead man if he try's any snake shit. I'll put a bullet right between his eyes if he do! Well pops since you don't know what's up with Tia I'll try to call her again. Martron I love you I'm sorry for being a fuck up when you were coming up. Some other time pops." The phone disconnected right on cue for Aujanique to enter the living

room. She looked like a caramel model strutting clad in her well put together outfit. " Hey Darren its good to see you. Same to you , looking like a dime piece. You're wearing them pumps baby. Tiffany we are gonna leave call me if you need me.Treyshawn and Deshawn come here."
Aujaniques twin sons stumbled into the living room play fighting. Towering their mother. Standing at 5"10 the boys had the stance of future NBA players. Light skin with red hair and freckles they looked more like Tiffany's siblings then nephews. They didn't favor their mother much. "What's up mama?" Treyshawn spoke he was the outspoken

one out of the twins. "Nothing I'm going on a date with Darren and I may be staying overnight."

D-Loc was surprised Aujanique spoke of possibly staying the night. The twins didn't mind they had been on a few outings with D-Loc taking a liking to him. The twins made plans to play basketball at D-Locs home in the near future.

Aujanique was eager to leave she wanted to enjoy herself in more then one way. Both Dloc and Aujanique were nervous. Listening to the sounds of Twista and Trey Songz "Girl Tonight" made them both have ideas they were to shy to share. He knew his dick game was good. Plus his money was long. "What bitch wouldn't want me?" He started to think as they pulled up in front of the restaurant. The two enjoyed their dinner both speaking nervously the entire time. Their date was lovely, they were both eager to find out what would happen, once they made it to his home. Once they reached his house. D-Loc was satisfied with the work his housekeeper had done. Rose petals were sprinkled on the ground. Slow R&B played smoothly on the stereo system. The mood was set the rose petals led from the foyer, to the master bedroom. The French doors were slightly ajar. There was a large boutique of roses on the nightstand, with a huge teddy bear and a jewelry box. That held a tennis bracelet and matching necklace. When Aujanique opened the box she was so grateful. She quickly laid D-Loc on the bed removing her heels. Stripping off her blouse,and her jeans. She quickly unzipped his pants pulling down his boxers. The shy role she was playing was out. Kneeling down she took inch by inch of his hard dick into her jaws,down her throat. She sucked and slurped as if his dick was a lollipop. D-Loc couldn't handle it for long. Grabbing a condom covering his erect tool. He entered Aujanique for the very first time. It felt like heaven her right walls gripped his dick while her juices covered it. The two made love throughout the night. Satisfied they fell asleep in each others arms.

The next morning Dloc had a proposition for Aujanique. "I'm really falling for you fast. And I love the hard worker you are. Baby you, the boy's, and your sister Deserve a better life. Move in with me. I promise to treat you like the queen you are and be there for all of you guys. I'm not trying to rush into anything Darren. We are already stable at my house. I know it's basic compared to this mansion but we are fine where we are at." D-Loc was somewhat hurt that Aujanique denied him. They were together everyday for two weeks straight.After the first night they stayed together.

The answer no Aujanique had given him quickly turned into a yes. Everything happened at a fast pace. Aujanique and her family had now became a part of Dlocs home. He was happy, overjoyed.He had never felt the dynamics of a real family. He was finally getting that in his mid 40s.

Chapter 6

Tia sat in the plush hotel suite, sipping Grey Goose.She listened to her Beyoncé C.D; poping two ecastsy pills. She was preparing herself for her next date.Tia had been In Las Vegas for two weeks.Quickly adjusting to her new life of hoen. It wasn't as bad as she imagined. Yes she was having sexual encounters with strangers. However she was making a killing. Madrix kept her under the influence of drugs and or alcohol. Most of the times she was on both. Her being numb made the whole process of prostitution feel normal.

The men came to see her, or she went to see them.They paid for the service, either they left or she returned to the hotel she was staying at. Madrix was right Tia was a gold mind. Making nearly ten thousand dollars in a weeks time. He instructed her on how to pick up customers in the casinos, the track and the websites that customers and sex workers set up dates, Backpage. He obtained her fake I.D that read she was 21 years old. Her ad also had the same information. Most customers would be to afraid to indulge on a visit with a minor openly. They would be afraid it was a sting to arrest them. She was told to not answer any block phone calls or tell any of the customers. Her exact location. Madrix coached Tia regarding screening her Incoming calls. She learned quickly. He didn't want any run ins with law enforcement. The best way he could avoid police contact was to do everything thru Tia to keep his hands clean.

 Tia was afraid when she first started out. After receiving $700 from her first lick, she was all for her new life style.after consuming the liquor and drugs she anxiously waited for her next date.

   The middle aged whit man

The middle aged white man knocked on the door to her suite. Handing her $800. "You are so beautiful." The man exclaimed. "What service would you like today? Full service please! That will be $1200. Tia knew how to tell a trick one price in a phone conversation, then switch It in person. He didn't object he gave her $300 to complete the transaction. He couldn't resist her she had batted her eyelashes while squinting her sexy green eyes.Tia did sexual acts with the man for thirty minutes. The trick dressed quickly handing Tia a 200 dollar tip.

 Tia showered quickly calling Madrix. " Hey baby, hey doll how much did you hit for? I made 1400, you are a bad ass bitch. In a year or so you can retire from the game." Madrix promised Tia she could stop in a year, he knew he was lying. Being a greedy pimp he would work her until he could no longer pimp her out. " We need to talk though meet me at the Mandalay Bay." Tia left the room promptly looking fly in a black Chanel see through romper, fluorescent pink lace pantie and bra set black and pink fluorescent stripper heels and Chanel shades to top it off. She walked up to Madrix in the lobby with her held down being in pocket as he had instructed her to do. " Come here baby you look sexy then a motherfucka blood." Madrix roughly kissed Tia. He could publicly do as he pleased with her outside of Portland. If they were home he wouldn't dare treat Tia the way he was. His homeboys wouldn't agree with what he was doing. Tia was Martrons sister, not only was she a hommies sister she was also underage. Madrix was foul in from every aspect. He had gotten the two of them a hotel room. Once they were behind closed doors Tia stripped out of her clothes to have sex with her pimp. " Hol' up bitch you looking good as fuck but where is my $1400?" Tia reached into her bra handing him the money. He was pleased, they quickly started to engage in sex. "Tia I want some slow neck." Tia laid him on his back sucking his dick the way he taught her.

He then bent her over sliding inside her cave unprotected. After they both climaxed. Madrix knew it was time he showed Tia his pimping in full affect.

"Tia I like the way you're working,thank you the shit is easy as fuck, but check this out Veda and my other bitches flying out here in the a.m. Why Madrix that's going to be drama." He knew having to conversation with her would be difficult. He was a pimp she wasn't his only hoe, Tia would have to get used to other women being around him. "I told you I like the way you getting this money. But I need all the paper I can get. I do have four other hoes. The show has just begun. It won't be no

drama because bitches know not to try me with
that type of shit. We can't be laying up fucking all
day. We gotta get this money.We gonna eat here
for a few more days . Then we going to New York.
My homeboy out there getting money. He sitting on
millions. I'm a nigga with a plan. I want to retire
with millions fuck a few 100 stacks. Niggas are
crazy doing this pimping shit forever. I'm tryna
open some strip clubs and do this shit legit.Baby
imma be the Scarface of their pimp game." Tia
wasn't sure what Madrix was saying was true. She
wouldn't dare question him. She felt everything he
had told her this far was correct. The next morning
at 10:00 am sharp.Madrix sat poolside at the

Mandalay Bay's beach like swimming pool waiting for the women to show up. Tia was the first to arrive.Clad in Louis Vuitton thong swimming suit with matching gladiator sandals, her hair weave braided into a single French braid displaying all of her beauty.Madrix sat beside her in a beach chair,rocking Louis Vuitton trunks. Veda walked up looking like a superstar. Wearing a Roberto Cavalli romper with wedged Jimmy chos heels. "Tia you all ready know Veda so y'all speak. Hey Veda, hey Tia." Madrix was irked by His babies mothers dry greeting. Her tone lacked enthusiasm. "Enough of you're attitude bitch I want the money you got for me. You're not going to ask about your son? Bitch he's at your moms I know that. Madrix was a poster child for deadbeat dads. His only concern was making more money. He made introductions with the other hoes. Tia met a white girl he simply called Snow which was such a cliche. Since white hoes were usually labeled snow bunny's. She was pale as a ghost ,very small and petite Snow had an angelic face no one would ever peg her as a prostitute. Tia was also introduced to Mahogany, she was a islander women. Tall standing at 6 ft, a true stallion . Her body was stacked in all the right places.He skin tone was a smooth Caramel , it appeared to be as soft as silk. Both of the women were friendly, down to earth

173

nothing like Veda. Madrix spoke to the women as if he was running a corporation.

"Okay ladies now that we have done the introductions. It's time to get down to business. We fucking with the casinos, the blade, the clubs and the net. Let's get this motherfucking money. We hitting New York next." Madrix departed with Veda. Tia and the other women left making their way to The Palms hotel. They were all sharing a hotel suite with two full size beds. All three of the women complained, knowing they made enough money to have their own hotel rooms. They all were following Madrixs' rules. He had expensive taste, he was also very cheap. Tia received a phone call from Madrix. " Aye I forgot to tell you if either one of them bitches do some weird shit don't tell me. Just out hoe them bitches. I hate a head ache ass complaining bitch. Make me see why you should be number one. All three of the women sat in the hotel room silent. Mahogany was an outspoken chick from The Bronx. She decided to take leadership and break the ice. Directing her conversation to Tia. " I see you new in the game ma?" Tia wondered how Mahogany knew that she was a beginner in the hoe game. She was a well seasoned hooker, Mahogany had saw it all, she could point a new hoe out in a crowded room. "Yes I just started a few weeks ago. Oh shit how old is you? I just turned 16." Mahogany was irked that Tia was a teenager. "That motherfucka Madrix! On my mother that's weird he got you hooking. I thought he was better then that. I started off when I was 13. Walking the streets of New York." Snow chimed In she had been thru the same struggle. "I started off when I was 12. I met Madrix two years ago. He upgraded my hustle, naming me Snow. Saying I favor Snow White." Mahogany laughed loudly. She had been on a few trips with Snow they got along well. They were initially silent when they met Tia. Assuming she was stuck up. Mahogany replied to Snows comment after she laughed for thirty seconds straight.

"Bitch he call you Snow because your ass is a coke whore! Mahogany shut the hell up you like blow too. Who said I didn't I'm numb when I'm out there in the field. Do you got some snow, Snow? Yep I got a 8 ball. Well bust that shit down." Snow removed a ziplock bag with a white substance Tia had never saw before. She took it out of the bag it was somewhat hardened. Using a razor to create small lines of the drug. She made 6 lines of the coke. Snow and Mahogany snorted two lines a piece up their nose. Mahogany looked at Tia inviting her in. "Yo you want a hit? I ain't never tried it. I only fuck with thizz." Mahogany shook her head. "Gurl ecastsy is cut with all type of shit heroine,meth,coke,molli. Yo just try it if you don't like the powder don't fuck with it no more." Tia took the 100 dollar bill that was rolled up. Bent her face down towards the table the lines of drugs were on ,Inhaling her first line of cocaine. She was on cloud nine taking on a different high then she had experienced before. Mahogany saw her eyes getting glossy. " You like that shit huh ma? Yes I do never felt so alive. Mahogany and Snow fed Tia line after line of coke. They snorted the lines likem there was no tomorrow. Mahogany and Snow started to grind on one another. It wasn't in a playful manner. More in a lustful sense. Tia was aroused, she was confused, she wasn't gay. Her pussy was feeling wet. Making her feel somewhat awkward. She ignored that feeling, enjoying the feeling of lust. Tia had been a part of a few threesomes with Madrix. The women weren't as attractive as Mahogany or Snow. The two women started to tongue kiss deeply. Mahogany started to finger Snows pussy. "Yes baby right there fuck me". Tia was enthralled by the two women enjoying one and other.Snow moved away from the encounter coming closer to Tia. Without hesitation Snow removed all of Tias clothing. Mahogany joined In laying Tia down. The two women then formed lines of cocaine on her abs snorting them. Mahogany bent Snow over engorging on her pussy as snow did the same to Tia. They enjoyed each other for two hours.

Once their rendezvous ended, Mahogany once again spoke as the leader. " Aye Tia don't discuss this shit with Madrix or what I'm about to do. I got regulars out her, four of them . They will pay me two thousand a piece. I will line up all my dates back to back. So we can all chill and relax for the night. Madrix ain't with us hella fucking and partying. He likes to link me and snow together because we make the most doe. Both of us are veterans we got regulars all across the country one day you will too. We get drunk, high, party, shop all day. We do this shit under his nose." All Tia did was nod her head she loved the way Mahogany moved. Sure enough in less the three hours Mahogany had eight thousand dollars. She had sent Tia and Snow to the mall and out to eat. While she handled business. Mahogany deposited a thousand of her proceeds. She put money into her account everyday in case of a rainy day. When she grew to trust Tia she would teach her how to tuck money from Madrix as well. She saw a lot of herself in Tia. Not wanting her to end up like her stuck in the streets. Mahogany was 28 she had been a prostitute for 15 years. It was taking a toll on her mind, body and her spirit. She couldn't believe she gave her profits to a man that was younger then her. It wasn't what she had worked for.

Madrix sat In his hotel room when he received a phone call from Martron. "What's good Madrix? Long time no talk my nigga. Nigga Its only been a week since I talked to you. How you doing bro? Bored as fuck, Veda getting in my nerves.Whats up with you out there in Cali though? Nothing my Baby mama Monica gettin on my damn nerves too fuck! I hate I missed Tia's birthday.Imma surprise her though I'm coming home." Madrix heart dropped that was not a part of his devious plan. "When are you planning on coming back? I'm coming tomorrow. The smoke finally clear with the feds I can come out there for sure. And I don't

fear the street shit at all.I spoke to my dad Imma

try to do the family shit. With him and Tia we

really need to reunite. Damn you coming back

tomorrow nigga?" Martron heard the fear in his

so-called friends voice. "Why you say it like that.

It's been to long since I saw my little sister. I

appreciate you being a step in big brother to her.

But it's about time I be the brother she need,

material shit ain't everything she need me. Im

catching a three a-clock flight. I will be there by

6pm Okay bro I got you! Pick me up Young P and

make sure you have some dro on you. Im tryna get

blazed I'm sick of this Cali weed. They be sleeping

on Portland's fire. Aye nigga I already said I got you. Can I talk to Tia before we hang up. Bro she went to the store. Oh okay tell her to call me from her phone when she gets back. Aight I'll see y'all tomorrow." Madrix was nervous he had to think fast. He quickly dressed. Speeding to pick up Tia he called her as he drove. Almost crashing into a stop sign on the way. When he arrived he was in panic mode. Telling Snow and Mahogany he would be back in three days, to report to Veda with the money they would make. Tia rushed out the hotel lobby not knowing what was going on. she was following Madrix instructions. He had told her to pack all of her things and to not ask him any questions. Once she was Inside the car, he drove to the airport. Madrix bought tickets for a straight flight to Portland. The plane would take off within a hour of their arrival. Madrix was lucky he found a convenient flight.They walked to the gate in the North Las Vegas Airport. Tia was wearing a revealing Fendi dress. She still played the in pocket role in the airport. Walking behind Madrix with her head down. They were spotted by Savy Cuz, a Portland Native whom was also a pimp. He couldn't wait to tell his O.G, D-Loc that his daughter was hoeing. Especially for Madrix. The news would shake shit up. Savy Cuz knew Matron would quickly turn on his best friend. There was no question that Madrix would die by the hands of Martron perhaps even D-Loc if they found out. Madrix was completely distracted by rushing to their flight, he did not notice Savy Cuz.

Once Madrix and Tia were seated. He explained to her. The change in plans. The unexpected arrival of her older brother. They would once again have to play the role of " big bro,lil sis". Madrix was aware of the fact that Tia was not paying attention to him. "Tia are you listening to me? Yeah, Why do I feel like you're not. I'm just tired Madrix, fuck no bitch your high. No I'm not, I don't have any more weed or pills." Tia was trying to pull one over Madrix head it was not working.

"Nah bitch your in powder. Look at your pupils, they are fucking huge. Fuck it we will deal with this shit another time. Right now I need you to act like a normal 16 year old kid." Madrix didn't realize how sick he sounded. " You gotta pretend to be sick so your brother doesn't wonder why you haven't been to school. Do you hear me? Yes I hear you." Tia suddenly felt sick rushing to the bathroom. Where she puked all over the toilet. She hurried cleaning it to the best of her ability. The plane was set for take off. She rushed back to her seat.Thinking about the fact that she hadn't had her period in nearly four months.She spotted a little, which was strange. Tia Ignored it, but she knew there was a possibility that she was

pregnant.

 They arrived to the PDX airport at 9:30pm. When

they made it to Tias condo. Madrix ran around

frantic. " Okay Tia make your bedroom look

childish . Decorate your walls with Pretty Ricky

posters. Put Ciara up there too. Madrix why do we

gotta front like this?" Tia was thrown off by his

behavior. He told her that all of his instruction was

right. Why was there a reason to hide anything.

"Why in the fuck wouldn't we front bitch? Your

becoming my star player , but right now you need

to get your mind off coke mode and focus bitch!"

Chapter

Martron arrived at the PDX airport excited to see his little sister and best friend. He walked towards baggage claim. Spotting Tia in a Nike sweat suit and Air Force Ones. She looked as innocent as could be. The siblings embraced with a huge, lasting hug. "Martron I missed you. Man sis I'm sorry Ive been gone for so long Imma make it up to you. I love you bro no worries. Madrix come here! Standing off to the side like I'm not gone acknowledge the way you been holding shit down. No problem blood this is our little sister." Madrix put his lie on thick, he had mastered multiple personalities. The three of them got into Tias Lexus merging into traffic. They all laughed as the inhaled the fumes of the purple Cush weed smoke. Martron was excited to be home, he wanted to be seen. He had laid low long enough. " Aye sis take me to the hood. Tia drove out of airport way on to 82nd Avenue. She drove up to Prescott street. Tia , Madrix and Martron were engulfed in conversation. Distracted, not noticing the black Toyota Camry following them.Tia pulled up to the four way stop on 60th and Prescott. Suddenly the Camry drove Up on the curb, on the passenger side of the Lexus. Several shots were let off penetrating the car like lightening. The shots rang out loudly from the Machine gun. Spraying the car terribly.

The Camry was occupied by one crip Ty.

He wanted pay back for the death of Stacey Jr.

He drove off swiftly merging into to traffic. Tia

screamed as she saw her brother slumped over in

the passenger seat. Madrix was also shot in the

shoulder. It was as if god had a angel cover her.

There wasn't a hair misplaced on Tias pretty head.

" Madrix call the ambulance my brother is going to

die. Tia shut the fuck up drive him to providence

they are going to take way to long to come." Both

Tia and Madrix reiterated what happened. When

D-Loc arrived.

Madrix has just had the bullet In his shoulder removed. He stood in a sling, as If being shit didn't faze him. Tia ran into her fathers arms. D-Loc did not embrace Madrix . He ignored him, having disliked Madrix since Martron was a teenager. He was a street nigga himself. There was just something cut throat about Madrix that he couldn't quite put his finger on. A tall white Male doctor approached Tia and D-Loc. "Mr Brandt your son suffered from ten gunshot wounds. He has made it out of surgery. However he is still not In a stable condition. We are going to house him In ICU. He is not coherent." Tia dropped to the floor passing out from the tragic news of her brothers state. " Hi Tia

I'm nurse Brandy you're at Providence hospital. You have been out for a while. You passed out. At one point you woke up kicking and screaming uncontrollably. We had to sedate you. You have been asleep for ten hours. We ran a few test on your blood with your fathers permission. Tia saw both D-Loc and Madrix standing behind the nurse. " Tia would you like to speak alone or in front of your family? What do you mean anything you have to say to me you can say in front of them." The nurse cleared her throat. Tia you have a positive pregnancy test." Tia passed out once again. When she woke up her father stood over her silent, he was disappointed. " Tia can you hear me? Yes daddy I can hear you. Baby girl what have you been doing? Just going to school and chilling. That's bullshit Tia. How In the fuck did you get pregnant? Has Madrix violated you baby? No not at all. Tia look me in my eyes and tell me that.Tia was to afraid to look her dad in the eyes and lie. "Is that grown ass slob nigga fucking you? No dad he isn't, your making this about gang stuff. No I'm not Im cool with some blood niggas respectable ones like your brother. But Madrix I don't fucking trust him,I never did. I'm going to be honest dad I only had sex once with Kevin. Hmmm one of Johnnys sons. That's why you were with him when he got hit. Y'all was thinking y'all was grown.Tia you just saved Madrix pitiful little life. You need to come stay with me." Tia was angered by D-Loc asking her to live with him. He had never played a big role In her life . " Hell nah I'm not moving in with you. You ain't shit but a sperm donor man." D-Loc didn't argue with Tia he hadn't been much of a father to her. " Sweetheart I know I didn't do a good job at being in you or your brothers life. I would at least like to be a better grandfather then I was a father. I said I'm not moving in with you!" D-Loc didn't want to take it there with his daughter but she had his back against the wall. "Tia you are still a minor your mother never had full custody over you. I signed the birth certificate.

Legally you have to live with me if I say so. Or you can get emancipated. As of right now your moving in with me." Tia could not believe her father was taking charge the way he was. He always seemed like a older homeboy vs. father. "Tia one more question why did they find cocaine in your system." Before she could answer the nurse walked in. They ran more test on Tia finding chlamydia in her system. D-Loc was more then disappointed in Tia. " So Johnny's son is a dirty nigga I see." He was cut off from the speech he was about to give. The nurse starter to apply a goopy substance to Tias stomach. It was cold, uncomfortable at first it quickly turned to her body temperature. When Tia looked at the screen she started to cry. She could hear the her babies heart beat. D-Loc grabbed her hand also shedding a tear. The nurse told Tia she was four months pregnant. Tia was convinced she was having a boy. Saying she saw a penis. D-Los feelings were feelings were mixed . He was upset that his daughter was young and pregnant. He was also willing to be there for her. He wanted to help with his grandchild. That way she could aspire to be all that she ever dreamed of. Madrix sat in the waiting room angry. Tia had only been a hoe for a few weeks and she was pregnant. That would surely slow down the plans he had in store. He didn't want anymore kids. He was afraid if the baby was his that his life would be on the line. He was correct. Both Martron and D-Loc would seek vengeance on him.

After Tias ultrasound, her and D-Loc joined Madrix in the waiting room. The three of them were escorted to Martrons ICU room. They saw Martron hooked up to several machines they all gasped. He didn't look like himself. His face was swollen from being shot in his Jaw. He looked weak, he looked hurt. D-Loc was the first to shed a tear. Although the two bumped heads. Martron was his only son. Grabbing his sons frail hand he spoke. " Son I know I've been a aint shit nigga, but I love the fuck outta you. You gonna make it baby boy I love you. I never tell you this but, In proud of you. For holding shit down, being a good father and always looking out for your little sister. You gonna make It son." D-Locs face was flooded with tears. Tia stood silently crying at her brothers current condition. Plus the news of her pregnancy made her sad.

" Aye Madrix take Tia to the little spot in the Pearl District. Make sure she pack all her shit and drop her off to my house. Okay I got you. What color was the car that rode up on y'all? It was black a Camry I think." D-Loc knew exactly who was driving the car. His little hommie Ty was the shooter. Family was first he would never pick his set over his son. D-Loc hugged Tia, kissing her on the forehead. Exiting the hospital making G calls. Shit was about to go down. Tia and Madrix caught a cab. The car was taking into evidence by the police. Tia was glad she didn't leave with her dad. She knew her and Madrix needed to talk. They didn't speak until they made it to the condo. Madrix was upset about Martrons condition. He also felt like the heat was off of him. Martron could not stop him, from pimping Tia if he died.

D-Loc was distracted by his sons shortcoming. Not able to focus on the situation his daughter was in. Madrix wasn't concerned with anything but his hustle. "Tia we gotta hop on a bird and go get this money." Tia was frustrated with Madrix how could he think about traveling when her brother was fighting for his life. "What the fuck are you talking about? My brother is fighting for his life. Bitch one monkey don't stop no show,definitely not stoping mines. If you wanna be broke and lay up by your brothers bedside. Then do it bitch I don't give a fuck. Calm down Madrix please. Tia how am I going to be calm when your pregnant? Kids are expensive. You're going to have to go harder now that your knocked up. That's just how shit works. Tia I hope we have a son." Madrix rubbed her belly, pretending like he wanted to be a father to get in her head. "Madrix I'm so scared, Don't be I got you. Imma fire Veda's ass you gonna be my main bitch love. We gotta get to the Big Apple so we can get this money baby.

Tia and Madrix quickly packed for their trip to New York. Tia did not want to live with her father. She wanted to hustle. Fearing she would not be able to take care of her child. If she did not listen to Madrix. Tia was ignorant to all the help she could receive from programs. She could also or get a job. Her father would help her. Her downfall was being a naïve 16 year old, involved with a grown man who was manipulating her for his own gain.

D-Loc was on a rampage. Aujanique and the kids could not comfort him. Once he tried contacting Tia to move in with him. He knew Madrix had played him for a fool. He pondered why he didn't go with the gut feeling he had, to murk Madrix. Martron had battled for his life. D-Loc was happy, he was overjoyed when he received the call that his son was out of the coma. D-Loc put a word out to the streets to look for Tia. Savy Cuz had allowed seeing Tia with Madrix in Vegas slip his mind. When he heard D-Loc was interested in her whereabouts. He was instantly reminded, about spotting her in Las Vegas. Savy gave D-Loc the evidence he needed. He had taken photographs of

Tia and Madrix. Although he was a pimp himself, Savy did not have dealings with under age girls. He had homeboys who had the same behavior as Madrix. He viewed them all the same, predators. Preying on young women wasn't something Savy viewed as respectable. Although Martron was indeed one of his enemies. He still knew he would murder Madrix for turning his kid sister out. D-Loc kept his cool. He knew Martron was in no position to find out, his best friend was pimping his Sister He knew Martron would blame himself. For leaving Tia in Madrix care. Martron was heavily medicated. He barley woke up. When he did he smiled at his father, said a few words passing back out into deep sleeps.

Martron would have to go to Physical rehab to recover from the gun shot wounds he suffered from. D-Loc received a phone call from the neighborhood, gossiping hood rat Rhonda. She was sneaky. The type of chick to set any nigga up, for a little bit of side money. " Dis D-Loc right? Yes who is this? Rhonda. Just the bitch I wanted to hear from. Yep yep it's me. you got any news for me? The nigga Ty hiding out at his mamas house on 8th and Skidmore.Well who all over there? Just him his mama and his two, nappy headed,ugly ass sisters. Okay thank you.Wait a minute how much you gonna pay me nigga? Or can I get some of that good ass dick I've been hearing about forever? Damn bitch I'll shoot you $500. You is a cheap ass nigga. Hol' up Rhonda you a fine ass bitch, I know your pussy good. But you'll have another nigga on the other end of the phone. Ready to kill me with your setup ass." D-Loc didn't pay Rhondas advances any mind. She was dangerous, she was messy. He would give her what he considered chump change. He knew he had to pay his little homeboy Ty a visit.

Dloc crept up in a bucket Pontiac grand Prix to the house on 8th and Skidmore. He was dressed in all black ready for a problem. His face was covered with a ski mask. He parked two blocks away, slow jogging to the house. He got out of the Pontiac. Ducking inside a bush in the front lawn near the porch.He knew a young hustler like Ty would leave during the night, to make moves. D-Loc waited for nearly an hour. Ty exited the front door. D-Loc pulled out his 45. Clocking Ty in the side of his head he knocked him out cold. Having strength D-Loc thru the young man over his right shoulder. Carried him to the car throwing him in the trunk. The streets were surprisingly quiet. He drove quietly to and abandoned warehouse in N.E Portland.When Ty awoke he was tied to a scraggly wooden chair.D-Loc stood over

Ty removing his mask. " What's up hommie what am I doing here? You should be asking yourself why you shot my son?" D-Loc yelled as he put a bullet in Tys left kneecap. Ty cried " Nigga I didn't shoot Martron! You think I'm stupid nigga? Wrong Answer." D-Loc removed a pocket knife from his back pocket. Slicing Ty's bottom lip off. Blood splattered all over the both of the men. " Say you ain't from Rolling bitch." D-Loc held his gun to Ty's head. Ty could not move his mouth to speak clearly. "Say it nigga, Say you ain't from motherfucking Rolling nigga." Ty said a silent prayer to god. D-Loc emptied the gun clip out. On his little homeboys head and torso area killing him. He left the warehouse he set the car and all

the clothing he wore on fire. He had tucked a

spare pair of clothes near the warehouse he got

dressed. Waking to his Bentley. He had previously

parked It three blocks away from the warehouse.

D-Loc was afraid to take a cab or the bus. He was

old school. He knew public transportation had

been upgraded. There were cameras on the

buses,trains and cabs. He felt the cameras were

tracking devices. Once he made It home. He was at

peace with what happened to his son. He knew

once his homeboys found out he killed Ty nobody

would question him. He had put in to much work

for anybody to question him. Martron was a blood

the Rolling 60's did not like him. Blood was still thicker then water to D-Loc. His new focus was now finding Tia and Madrix. He would kill him on sight.

Martron spoke on the phone with Cynthia. " So you den made it to the pen baby? Yes I got here yesterday, them bitches already tryna be your girlfriend huh? Hell nah stop it! Did you get that joog I sent you? Yes I got it thank you so much.I want you good in there. don't worry about me my mom is looking out for me. I owe you love! Cynthia call me back its breaking news. Okay I'll call you at my next Day room." Martron was shocked as his eyes were glued to the tv screen. " Breaking news in N.E Portland. A 19 year old African American man was found murdered. In this dilapidated warehouse by a homeless couple. The victim was shot multiple times and mutilated. The victim has been identified by his family . As 19 year old Tylique Roberts. Portland police believe the death is gang related. Please contact The Portland Police or Crime Stoppers with any tips regarding this case. Back to you Tim on the weather."

Martron had saw Ty pull the trigger to the gun that shoot him. He was shocked when the news caster spoke while they displayed Tys Oregon I.D photograph. Martron smiled ear to ear thinking to himself. " Madrix my nigga he got that bitch ass crab nigga." Not knowing his father was the one who had handled the situation for him.

Chapter 8

Tia had been to three states in a two week time period. Traveling with her wife in-laws Mahogany and Snow, who spoiled her as best as the could because she was pregnant. Mahogany had four children. All of her kids were trick babies. She still was against Tia drinking or smoking while she was pregnant. The women had made it to Atlanta, making a killing in both New York and Texas. "Tia what are you going to name your baby? I don't know yet Madrix said name him Currency. Hell nah don't name him that name him Andrew." Snow didn't have children but she believed she thought of the best names .Mahogany laughed at Snows name choice. She wanted to help her wife in-law name her child. " Tia what are your favorite things? I love clothes , I love food." Mahogany rolled her eyes her children were all named after months. April, May, August and December. She liked to name children in themes. Coming up with the names because she loved making it to see another year. Mahogany told Tia her children's names. Tia thought for a moment. My favorite movie is The Lion King. If I have a girl I could name her Nyla if I have a son I can name him Simba. Both me and Madrix think it's a boy." Tia did not want to spell the names correctly she wrote

on a piece of scratch paper . Nyelah and Symbah.

Mahogany looked at Tia with sorrow in her eyes.

Knowing her child would end up either with her

father, brother or in the system. Mahogany spoke.

" Tia look I told you I have four kids. I save lil'

change on the side and send my kids three

thousand a month, damn Mahogany you're a good

mom. Tia no I'm not they have no mother my

mama is raising them. I'm out here hooking while

they growing up with no mother or father. I sneak

off to see them whenever we go to New York.

Madrix would never just let me go to see them. He

doesn't give a fuck about no kids not even his

own. He's a greedy con artist motherfucka." Tia was angry with Mahogany about her rant. She wanted to black out on her instead of letting the situation escalate. Tia questioned her. "If he so greedy why do you fuck with him then? Why do you keep paying the nigga?" Tia spoke sharply. "Bitch I use to ask myself the same thing. But I'm a hustler. I've been In the game for 15 years. There ain't shit I haven't done or saw. I've been raped, beat down,robbed. Even by some of my old pimps. I'm more game tight then Madrix. The confrontation is light weight. Madrix is still a dirty dog. But I like fucking with him becausee I can tuck money. I got over 100 grand saved up.Well if you got all that money, why are you still hoen Mahogany? Im a hustler like I said lil' bitch. Imma stop when I have a million dollars stacked up. Open myself a chain of salons and shit." Tia could see the sparkle in Mahogany's eyes when she talked about her goal. She could hook up any hairstyle. She was beyond talented. "Tia I'm letting you in on this. Because I see so much of myself in you. I don't want you to end up like me. Four kids later on the blade ma. I've walked the streets until my feet bled. Ain't shit sweet about this shit. It's just all I know. I'm nothing like you Mahogany! Tia you better chill out. And wake the fuck up you think you better? The nigga in your head that much that you think you the top bitch.

He still go Veda lil' girl. That's his wifey the bitch

ain't going no where." Snow had been quiet the

entire discussion. Shit was heating up, drama gave

her bad anxiety. She chimed in. "Mahogany stop

she's just a baby. I know that, that's why we can't

sit back and let the nigga fuck her mind up. Fuck

that shit Yo!" Tia received a call from a trick. She

set up the date easily. Mahogany was done

preaching. She was lost cause. It was money time.

"Tia you got a date? Yes I have to meet him at The

Hyatt Hotel. I have to meet him in thirty minutes.

Well me and snow are gonna go do a two girl date

with this regulars I got out here. Make a little two

thousand. You know how I do it Tia!" Mahogany was excited to do the date with Snow. She never had slept with Madrix she loved pussy. Becoming infatuated with other women during the years she spent in the game. "Tia call Madrix and let him know where your lick is at. Okay I will, cool we finna bounce we will see you later.

Tia touched up her makeup. She had forgotten to make the phone call to Madrix. She strutted out the Hotel lobby. Getting inside the Ford Focus Madrix rented for her. She did not even look a day pregnant. The pregnancy did give her a beautiful glow. Her skin was clear and smoother then ever. Her weave was in tact down her back. She rocked an excessive amount of Mac makeup on her face. She wore a skippy purple strapless dress from H&M. Tia was fabulous with her attire. But she still wore cheap shit from time to time. Her outfit was finished off by purple Guess sandals. Tia parked in the uncovered visitor parking area. In the Hyatt hotel parking lot. Calling her date. "Hey you what room are you in? Oh honey I'm so glad you have arrived I'm in room 310." Tia stepped on to the elevator feeling odd. An awkward cramp floated thru her stomach . She thought the feeling was a nervous butterfly. She had never been to Atlanta before. Tia didn't know how the tricks behaved in the south. She knocked on the hotel room door. A tall white man opened the door. "You are so beautiful." He spoke to Tia in a lustful tone. As soon as Tia entered the room. The man reached over her slamming the door. He then hit Tia in her face. With a closed fist, Tia dropped to the floor. He dove for both her purse and her cell phone. Throwing them closer to the door. He kicked Tia in the face. Pinning her down to the floor. Tearing off her dress; Tia cried out on pain. The man removed the jeans he wore. Pulling his boxer briefs down. Ripping Tia's lace thong off of the bottom half of her body. He entered her body roughly. His dick wasn't large. Tia still felt a major amount of pain. He thrust in and out of her causing her to start bleeding from her vagina. He climaxed Pulling his pants up. He took Tia's belongings , leaving her crying on the hotel room floor. Tia mustered up strength to pull herself up from the ground. She made it to the the hotel lobby. Where the clerk called the police. The clerk gasped while on the phone. Tia had two black eyes and a busted lip. Blood trickled down her legs. "Please help me I have been raped and I'm pregnant. I'm on the phone with the police as we speak.They are going to help you." Tia thought about the police connecting her to Madrix. She decided to take herself to the hospital. Weakly walking out of the hotel doors. The clerk chased behind her. Tia made it to the car, she wasn't able to move as fast as she wanted to get away from the hotel. The clerk was able to tell the police the license plate number to the Ford Focus.

Tia did not know Atlanta well, she was still able to find Emory Universal Hospital. She was quickly treated. Her main concern was her child. She put the rape out of her mind. Not wanting to relive it. The nurse who had done her rape kit spoke calmly to her. "Ms.Brandt your baby Is okay. You have some breakthrough bleeding.But we have to keep you to monitor the both of you.We will keep you for 24 hours. I can't stay here." Tia argued, she believed she had her child's best interest. She was far from a concerned parent. Tia was a lost young girl. "Ms. Brandt we can not let you leave. Also the Atlanta police found a school I.D for you in the hotel lobby. You're attacker dropped it on his way out of the door. They would like to speak with you." Tia was beyond nervous. There was no way she could escape the nurse walked out of her hospital room as the police entered it. Two uniformed officers walked into the hospital room. They were both black which was surprising to Tia. Most of the officers Tia saw in Portland were white. Being in Atlanta was a culture shock to her on many different levels. The taller of the two officers approached her bed with a notepad. He was caramel complexed. He looked to be in his early 20s, he looked kind. "Hey there Ms. Brandt I'm officer Carl Williams. We didn't only find your school I.d card we also found your wallet. Inside contained several different fake I.d's with your name on Them. Your wallet contained Identification from, Washington, Nevada, New York,Texas, Georgia and California. Can you give me and explanation why you have so many fake I.d's?" Tia sat quiet as a church mouse. " That there black eye is why I need you to be honest with me. Your school I.d showed you are a minor. I've been in contact with authorizes in Portland. They confirmed that you're only 16 years old. I was informed that you had police contact because the death of your mother some months back?" The officer held his head down . " I'm sorry for your lost. Why are you asking me so many fucking questions? I'm going to be frank with you under age sex trafficking is at large down here in Atlanta. What are you trying to say?" Tia spoke as if she were truly offended. " What I'm saying Is I know you didn't just fall into this mess. The hotel clerk called us. We rushed to the hotel responding as fast as we could you were gone. You had contact with a strange man In a hotel room. This doesn't look good. You're a victim. I am not trying to point fingers at you, only trying to help you."

Tia was afraid she could not call Madrix or her
wife in-laws. She could not think of anything to do.
Tia was under a extreme amount of stress. All she
could think about is what Madrix told her to do if
she was ever questioned by the police. "If you ever
get jammed by the police. Just ask for a attorney."
Madrix wanted to prey on Tia as much as he could.
He was not only foul in the justice system. He was
foul as a man, he was disrespecting his hood, he
was an unloyal friend. Madrix was a predator.
Keeping Tia isolated was a way to control her. Tia
snapped back to the fucked up predicament she
found herself in. Pregnant, raped, hoen being
questioned by the police. " Tia I know you think

226

we are your enemy but we just want to help you."
The officer wanted to be less formal by calling Tia
her first name he thought he would be able to get
her to talk . "You can't help me with shit I need a
lawyer. We can help you. No man that loves you
would share you with any other man, nor would
he share you with dangerous strangers. Well since
you won't comply. Who can we contact to come
down here and get you? I know your mother
passed away. So who can I call that can come take
you home safely. Tia thought long and hard. She
had always leaned on her brother. She didn't
know what condition he was in. Tia had selfishly
left her brother while he was still comatose. He

was in no condition to save her and she knew he

was not. Tia thought about a Aunt she had in Texas

but she didn't know the women's number. It would

be difficult to contact her father. She didn't even

call him when she found her mother dead. She

assumed he was hot in the streets and had

warrants. Tia could tell by the last time she saw

him. That D-Loc had turned over a new leaf. Tia

broke down, she would be in for a rude

awakening with her dad. He would surely want to

kill Madrix. "You can call my father, Okay Tia I'll

call your father what's his name and phone

number?" Officer Williams ripped off a piece of

paper from his notepad. Tia gave the information

up. " Now Tia I want to warn you . Being that your under age I'm going to have to tell your father the truth. You don't have to tell him shìt. I'm a mandatory reporter it's my job yes I do."

Tia was frustrated but she had no other outlet. "Okay please call him so he can come get me out of here." D-Loc sat at his dinning room table eating smothered chicken breast, mustard greens, macaroni and cheese, yams and peach cobbler. Cracking jokes laughing at Treyshawn's humor. Aujanique, Tiffany and the twins brought a new light into his life. He was full of regret, that he didn't have a real family with his own children. Aujanique constantly asked about Tia's whereabouts. She thought it would be perfect for Tia to move In. Tiffany would have someone to hang out with. Dloc eyes watered up each time he thought about his only daughter. He always bragged about Tia to Aujanique. He had not gone into detail regarding the recent events of her pregnancy, or the fact that she was missing in action. He told Aujanique that Tia was being somewhat rebellious. D-Loc said she was staying with different friends. When his girlfriend inquired about where Tia was exactly. He would change the subject. D-Loc was clever by the way he handled his emotions publicly. He grabbed more chicken when his phone rang. He looked at his phone seeing an Atlanta area code. " Hold up y'all I gotta take this call somebody calling me from The A." Aujanique raised her eyebrow who could be calling her man from Atlanta? "Aujanique don't look like that it's probably somebody calling the wrong number. May I speak to Mr Brandt? Yes this is him hello. Hi sir I'm officer Williams with the Atlanta police. Your daughter Tia Is currently detained, what the fuck Tia's in jail?" D-Loc screamed loudly. Aujanique and the children all tuned in. They wanted to know what was going on, on the other end of the phone call. "No sir your daughter is not in jail. She was brutally raped and beaten at The Hyatt hotel down here in Atlanta .We found her wallet when she tried to leave before we could respond. There were multiple fake I.Ds from different cities sir. What the fuck you cant be serious. Please don't cut me off Mr. Brandt I know this situation is hard for you. However it's very serious. I believe Tia is involved In some form of sex trafficking. What the fuck you trying to call my baby girl a hoe. She is a victim if she is involved Im not calling her any names sir. I know I can't tell you to calm down continuously. I would be livid if I was in your position. I was instructed to take Tia into custody and contact child services. But I'd rather you guys not go thru all that. She's holding back not talking but I know she was being trafficked." D-Loc couldn't believe his ears. He thought to himself. " That slob ass, bitch ass nigga Madrix. Dirtbag motherfucka." He didn't take into consideration all the women he had preyed on in his days of pimping. "Where is my daughter? She Is right here in the hospital bed. I will not allow her to leave the state unless you come to get her. I'm being unorthodox by not taking her in to the station. But she's been through enough. I'll be there ASAP you don't have to worry. Please come prepared to stay throughout the day. Tia can not discharge from the hospital right away. I don't know if you're aware that she is pregnant. Yes I know. Well she is pretty beaten up the child is alive. Thank god! But doctors and nurses want to make sure both Tia and the unborn child is okay. Mr. Brandt if you are not here within the next 48 hours I will have to release Tia to child services. Don't even say that I'll be there. May I speak to my daughter." The officer handed Tia the phone .She was afraid of everything she knew her dad would ask her. Yet she needed him more then ever. " Hey dad, hey baby girl. Are you okay baby? No dad I'm not." Tia broke down sobbing. " Daddy please don't tell Martron. I will let you do that just get some rest I will be there to get you okay baby. Okay dad." D-Loc ended his conversation with his baby girl in rage. All the occupants of the house knew there was trouble ahead.

Aujanique I need you to take off work for a few days, book us some flights to Atlanta that leave as soon as possible. I need to speak with you alone." That was the kids code to leave. They all grabbed their dinner plates exiting to their bedrooms. The kids wanted to be nosey. They wanted the scoop on the drama. "Aujanique Tia has been raped. By who Darren?" D-Loc took a deep breath he hated speaking about anything that associated with his past. "Aujanique there's a lot I haven't told you about myself. All this nice shit I got from pimping. Please don't judge me because I've changed. I was introduced to the shit when I was young. It's really all I know. I retired from the game when I was 39, I made enough doe and I was just tired of the shit. This Is my karma though I believe Tia was raped by a trick. My baby girl is getting pimped on."

D-Loc broke down wailing like a small child. Aujanique held her man as he let out loud sobs. She had heard about his reputation. Never questioning him, he never exposed that side of himself to her. She had never once saw the pimp or gang member D-Loc. From the day she met him.She knew only Darren. Aujanique Was a real ass bitch, She was loyal. She was ready to hold the man that she had grown to love Down.

" Aujanique , imma kill madrix, isn't that Martrons best friend? That nigga ain't no friend to my son. Underneath his watch. My daughter. Has contracted STD, gotten pregnant, came up missing and now she's laying up in a hospital bed raped." It was shocking to hear all the horrible events that had happened in Tia's life. "Darren, why in the fuck aint she here then? You're her father! Look it's complicated. Martron has been more of a father to my babygirl then I have ever been. When Nyemiah passed shit got hot for my son. He had to leave. He left Tia with Madrix, thinking he could trust the snake ass nigga. I didn't know right away. By the time I found out I was mad as hell. I was bamboozled. It seemed like Tia was doing really well the times that I spoke with her. She was playing me the whole time. Darren you should had physically checked on her . I tried she would never let me come to her. I know it's because I've put them kids thru hell. I understand why they hate me. When I met you I knew your kids and your sister would be the family I missed out on. I had the chance to build a family with my own children. But I ruined it by running the streets. Tia coming to stay with us is going to be a blessing. I can show her how much I've changed. She will want to be a part of my life too." D-Loc continued to cry, Aujanique held him. She was upset that he had

been a deadbeat father to his children. She had
been a single mother before the two of them got
together. She knew how kids that grew up without
fathers felt. She was angry with D-Loc. It wasn't the
time to discuss the mistakes he had made as a
parent any further. Aujanique booked two straight
flights to Atlanta. They would board the plane at
7:25am.

Chapter 9

Officer Williams checked on Tia the whole night
and the next day. He saw a future for Tia. If she
separated herself from hoen she could be great in
life. He was surprised by how smart she truly was.
He could tell she was not to far gone in the street

life. Tia still had a chance to be whatever she inspired to be. Tia was watching The Maury show when her father arrived. He walked into her room with a beautiful women she had never saw. "Tia baby oh my god look at your face." He rushed to her holding her while she shed big tears on to his Lacoste button down shirt. "You must be officer Williams? Yes sir I am. Thank you so much for looking out for my daughter." D-Loc didn't want to discuss Madrix in front of the cop. He was still a G and the plans he had for Madrix were far from him getting arrested. He wanted to murder him. D-Loc formally Introduced Tia to Aujanique. Tia was impressed she didn't look or speak like the women she had ever saw with her father. She wasn't

ghetto or hoodratish at all.

Aujanique left the hospital, checking into a

quiet hotel room to rest. D-Loc stayed by his

daughters bed side. He watched her rest ,when she

was awake he talked to her deeply. He wanted to

truly get to know his daughter. Both Tia and her

unborn child were okay. She was released into her

fathers care. D-Loc, Aujanique and Tia all boarded

their flight to Portland, on a sunny day In Atlanta.

D-Loc still had pimp partners In Atlanta he had

niggas on the hunt for Madrix. Mahogany and

Snow drove around Atlanta after four days of

searching overwhelmed and stressed. Mahogany was ready to leave Madrixs stable.

He had departed when she told him Tia was missing he left Atlanta to Philadelphia with Veda. Forcing her to make up a lie that she had a ten thousand dollar two girl date scheduled out later in the week. Ten thousand was a lot of money to lie about. Mahogany would withdraw it from her private account and pay Madrix. Tia meant the world to her. She saw to much of herself in the hopeless young girl. Mahogany had called the Atlanta police station. Tia wasn't in adult or juvenile custody. She did not take the time to call the hospitals. She went to the Hyatt hotel. Where she didn't get any information. Believing she was judged by the blonde wig she wore,with a leather body suite making her look like a exactly what she was a street walker. The two women were restless from their search. " Snow where in the fuck is Tia man? I hope she's not fucking dead out here Mahogany. Shut the fuck up Snow don't think like that. Maybe the trick she went to see was a weirdo. He could had kidnapped her. It's been four entire days. What are we going to do Mahogany? I told Madrix the made up lick Is a few days from now. We got two days to keep looking. We know she didn't choose up with another nigga. We got to put our ears to the streets and find out what's going on with Tia.

Chapter 10

Shit was definitely about to hit the fan in Portland. Martron would be cleared to leave the hospital within two days of his families return from Atalanta. D-Loc had hired his son a live in nurse. He didn't want all the weight of taking care of Martron to be on Zayley.All of Martrons trap spots had closed down when he went to California. He would had stayed at one of his spots. But his home with Zayley was the only option he had other then his father. Martron did not interact with any of his distributors. He was the supplier he had the connect. His lil hommie Tobbie handled all of the hand to hand business. He had also shut down all the trap spots. Renting new storage spaces to hold the product and the money. Tobbie was a low key nigga. He didn't speak much, he was more about action. He was only 18, young to most but Martron trusted him. Tobbie was a D-Boy at heart. Starting off his career in saling drugs at the age of 11. In downtown Portland, he moved up from a corner boy, to a mule , to a right hand lieutenant. He knew one day he would be the boss. He was patient not in a rush to compete with the man he looked up to more then anybody. Martron was a hero to Tobbie he would never say it out loud. He looked up to his older hommie. Tobbie did good

business. Other drug dealers knew he was legit

"That nigga" when it came to buying work. He

was 5,9 Light skin tone, with a scar across his left

cheek, from a stabbing that happened years back.

Martron's mind was heavy with thoughts. He

wanted to be there for his children. He knew he

had to look out for Tia she was like one of his kids

they had always been close. He wanted to buy

Cynthia a house. So she could be comfortable while

she got on her feet when she got out of prison.

Martron wanted to get healthy again. His street

goal was to paint the city red until he murked

David it bothered him that David murdered his

dear friend . Although Martron openly called David

a bitch. He knew deep in his heart the nigga would

get crazy too. Plus the Hoover's stuck together

with one another. If Martron killed David he would

be up against their whole set. He wasn't afraid. He

would seek revenge for the death of his homeboy.

Martron tried to contact Madrix. He wanted to

thank him for looking out for his sister when he

was gone. He thought it was odd that Madrix had

never checked up on him. While he was in the

hospital. And was not answering his phone calls.

He was grateful that he trusted his right hand man

to take care of his sister . In his eyes D-Loc wasn't

shit. Martron often shielded Tia from their father.

Afraid of what he could subject her to being a

pimp at heart. Feeling as if he had the chance he

would sale Tia himself. Martron held Madrix to a

different standard. He knew his homeboy would

never cross those lines. Martron decided to call

Madrix as he flipped thru the tv channels. The

phone was answered on the last ring by Veda. Her

tone was brash. "Hello! Hey Veda chill out where

Is Madrix as at? Oh he right here hold up." Veda

handed Madrix the phone with a slick grin on her

face. He had been engulfed in his Madden 2k6

video game to notice who she had been speaking

to. Veda knew she was forbidden from answering

Martrons phone calls. She had answered out of

spite. Wanting to start drama between her child's father and his best friend. Veda was growing to hate Madrix for always treating her like nothing but his hoe vs. the mother of his child. "Somebody wanna talk to you daddy, yo who ? This Mar Ru nigga what's good with you?" Madrix was shaking in his boots. The last person he wanted to talk to. He gave Veda an ice grill mug. She knew he told her not to answer Martrons calls. Madrix spoke nervously, "There's not much going on with me. Why is your voice trembling nigga are you okay? Yep I'm fine bro how are you? How's your health? I'm great man blessed for real for real. Blood we almost thought we lost you." Madrix secretly wished MarTron would had died. He was in a trance of fear. He realized he needed to think on his toes when Martron brought up Tia. "Have you talked to Tia ? Nah I haven't I was just about to ask you the same thing. Yep that's hella weird. When the last time y'all talk. About a week ago she's been missing in action. Where the fuck is my sister!" Martron shouted. "Man relax I don't know. How am I post to relax when your saying you haven't talked to her in a motherfucking week. Nigga you post to be looking out for her.Have you spoke to your pops. Briefly he's been up here to see me. He got me a live in nurse for Zayley house and shit. Guess what nigga? What? Did my dad tell you Tia pregnant. Is she? " Madrix played the role of innocence although he knew the child could possibly be his. " Yes she is knocked up by the lil snoove nigga Kevin." Madrix was glad Martron thought Kevin was the father. He would never indicate himself as a possible father. He knew his friend would take his life without hesitation. Martron ran out of words to say. He had vowed to protect Tia. Now he didn't know where she was or how she was doing. He felt he failed her. " Martron are you there? Yeah blood. I'm just trying to figure out how this shit happened. Like how did Tia end up pregnant? Don't blame yourself nigga. She was vulnerable as fuck after her mom died."

Nothing was making sense to Martron he knew Tias

ex boyfriend had been in the hospital during

Nyemiahs funeral. He thought she must had gotten

pregnant right before her mother was buried.

Martron was proud of his friend Madrix. Tia

running off was not his fault. He had done all he

could do. Taking own the responsibility of a

teenage girl. Who was of no relation to him was

beyond solid. If Matron knew the truth he would

think the total opposite of Madrix. "Well bro get at

me if Tia checks in with you, for sho." Martron sat

in his Jordan sweat suit pants, shirtless. The

hospital bed was not comfortable. He called his

dad angry with him as he usual. "Hey son how are

you? Nigga don't hey son me . You forgot to mention the news about Tia. I just talked to Madrix." D-Loc was caught off guard. He wondered how Madrix had swindled his way out of a problem with his son. D-Loc had told Martron Tia was pregnant. He didn't get into detail regarding what happened in Atlanta. He wanted his son to recover stress free. " Wait a minute son. I need to talk to you face to face I'm on my way up there." D-Loc hung up the phone before his son could respond. Twenty minutes had passed. Martrons red Motorola Razor cell phone rang. His fathers ring tone Tupac "only god can judge me", sang out. "What dad? I was just calling to tell you I'm outside parking my car.

D-Loc walked into Martrons hospital room with Tia by his side. Martron would had jumped out of the hospital bed if he could. More then happy to see his sister. "Pops what's going on how in the hell did you find Tia?" D-Loc was shocked that Matron. How did he know Tia had got been missing . He didn't know of the lie that Madrix had told him. "Boy the Atlanta police called me to get my daughter and I did. What the fuck you mean the Atlanta police called you?! I'll let your sister explain her own story." Tia was nervous. She had told her father multiple lies. Denying Madrixs' involvement. Tia was about to tell her brother lies

as well. She wanted to protect the man she loved.

Tia never planned on falling for Madrix. Things

had turned out that way without her trying. "

Martron please don't be mad at me. I'm listening

Tia I won't get mad. Well when you got hit I found

out I was pregnant . I didn't want to live with

daddy. So I went to Atalanta to stay with my

homegirl Tasha who graduated last year. One day

when she was at school I went on a walk. I met

this guy I thought he was cool. He asked me if I

wanted to smoke some weed. I know I shouldn't

be smoking but I said yes. We went to A hotel. He

went crazy beat me up and raped me. I got away

went to the hospital. The police came to see what happened. I had them call daddy to come get me." Martron never knew Tia to be a liar, but her story was full of holes. "Tia do you think you're grown blood?" Tia knew her brother was upset. He sat calmly,it was the look he gave her that showed his disappointment. He stared right into her green eyes. " Tia who are you pregnant by? Kevin. Where is he at then. He should be around helping you out. He don't fuck with me he think I set him up to get shot. Fuck all that he's going to take care of my niece or nephew. Who paid for you to fly to Atlanta. I know most college students don't got it like that to just be flying people out. I paid for it myself Martron I've saved all my money since I was younger. I know this is hard for you Tia. But a random man just beat you up and violated you? Was the man black, white,Mexican,Asian? He was white. Tia Why would you agree to go smoke with a random white dude. Even if he was black race don't got shit to do with being sloppy." D-Loc interjected with his own theory that he had been trying to get out of Tia. " Baby girl be honest. I know you don't deal with me like that. But your brother has always been there for you. At least tell him the truth. What do you mean dad I told the truth. Tia stop fucking fronting." Martron was lost in the conversation. "Pops what the fuck is she lying about? When they told me to come get her.

They told me Tia was a victim of sex trafficking.

Tia is lying about everything Cuz! The nigga that

you left to look after her been pimping on our

princess. The officer that I spoke with out there

was for sure that she was hoen. This shit is

unbelievable. Blood this shit is brazy. Son I didn't

tell you because I wanted you to be home

comfortably. I didn't want to stress you out . Tia's

pregnant and shit. Nothings adding up. Your sister

also tested positive for the clap. Madrix Is a dirty

mothafucka. Martron he's a snake! He's a pimp son

this shit ain't adding up. Your boy was fucking Tia,

he was pimping her too. And imma body him."

Martron was weak, he somehow mustered the strength to jump up from the bed . He yelled in his fathers face. "Madrix is my fucking bro! He would never do no shit like that to my sister blood. You ain't never been there for her. Now you wanna come around with all these theories. Fuck you! Tia ass pregnant by the snoove nigga. That's who we need to hunt down. Quiet as it's kept that's probably who she chasing around."

D-Loc was disgusted by Martrons ignorance. "Nigga you must be more medicated then you should be. It's obvious your slob ass homeboy the one orchestrated all of this." Martron was annoyed by the drawn out conversation. "Aye Tia when I get out this hell hole you coming to stay with me.

You're still going to graduate you're still going to

be something. Son so much has gone on. You're

sister dropped out of school." Martron had had

enough. He grabbed the collar of Tias half jacket.

" Why would you do that dumb ass shit sis. You're

so smart. Even I graduated from high school. I had

to because I got pregnant." D-Loc was irate by thr

constant lies. "Tia stop lying. I talked to your old

principal. You been dropped out months ago.

You're ass dropped out to hoe!"Martron was past

being angry. He was hurt confused. Pointing all

the blame at Kevin, turning a blind eye to Madrix.

He would do whatever it took to fix his sisters recent fuck ups.

" Dad I don't know why you're trying to make it out like Madrix is like you. He's nothing like you pops." D-Loc stared at his son in awe. He couldn't believe what he was hearing.

" I know I've been a aint shit nigga. But don't ever compare me To Madrix we are two different species. He's a bitch ass nigga, a sucka, a coward." Martron wanted to speak to his father alone. " Tia can you step out for a minute?" Tia exited the hospital room gladly. She was exhausted from lying. " Dad who got on Ty? Me of course you my baby boy before anything. Dad I knew it was you." Martron lied. "Thank you for taking care of that for me.. No problem you know I'm always going to have your back. Son what made you think it was me that took care of him. You my pops despite our differences. I know you're a vicious, hood nigga. I learned all my killa ways from you even though you a crab." Martron chuckled as he insulted his father being a crip. "Son I really want Tia to come stay with me. I'm in a relationship now. My life is way different. I want her to come with me to Zayleys house. Dad we should let her stay in the condo she got. She's about to be a mother. Hell nah she is going to need help. She is still a child my child. I don't think it's in her best interest to stay anywhere alone. Look what just happened to her."Martron and D-Loc were hustlers, killers. They could never just live freely. They had to worry about the opposition, warrants or the law. Neither D-Loc or Martron wanted Tia engulfed in the lifestyle of the streets. Martron agreed to let Tia stay with their father. Dloc took Tia to the condo she had In the Pearl district. She packed majority of her clothing. DLoc walked around the condo looking for evidence that Madrix had sexed Tia. He couldn't find any. Tias Lexus was ruined m during her brothers shooting. She was happy that her father had bought her a Beamer. She would need transportation to get to her appointments. Once father and daughter made It to the plush Mini Mansion. Tia was introduced to Aujanique and the kids. Tia and Tiffany Instantly clicked. They both had grown up without parents for the most part, they were the same age and both book smart. Not liking supervision Tia convinced Tiffany to sneak out the house with her. They made it downtown to the condo in the Pearl District within 15 minutes. Neither D-Loc or Aujanique noticed their departure. The two girls stepped out of the Beamer walking Into the condo. They chilled in the living room watching the film "Set It Off". Martron has a feeling that Tia would disobey their father and leave. He wondered if

Madrix was involved. He wondered whether or not they would meet at the condo.

Martron sent Tobbie to the condo. Knowing Madrix he knew there would be a few sets of Spare keys inside a fake flower plant outside the condo. Martron always thought his friend was sloppy for leaving keys in a plant. He knew Madrix wasn't the sharpest. Tobbie easily found the keys to the crib. The condominiums were individual units. He walked in finding Tia there. She wasn't with Madrix, she sat next to a light skin girl, with red hair and bright red freckles. Tobbie like Tiffany's look, he thought she was beyond fine. She was beautiful and he wanted her. He had no idea that she was battling with her sexuality. Having mixed emotions about men and women, she had a distinguishe preference. Tobbie spoke to Tia, he instantly started to spit game at Tiffany. " Aye beautiful what's your name? Tiffany. What's good with you with your fine ass can I get the number tho? Uh no I don't even know you. And I don't date thugs. Fuck you then bitch, I don't date stuck up bitches." Tia wanted Tobbie to leave, he was throwing off the vibe. "Tobbie what are you doing here? Your brother sent me. Well can you leave? Ain't you post to be at your dads? Yes we just wanted to kick it over her for a little bit . Well imma shake then fuck both y'all tho." The two

teenage girls finished watching "Set It Off",
deciding they wanted to watch the film "Belly".
They quoted The rapper Nas and DMX lines. The
two girls heard loud music near by. The girls
stepped on to the balcony. Noticing a handsome
brown skin cat standing on the balcony of the
condo that was located next door. The man saw
them watching him. He yelled over the loud music.
"What's good with y'all ? Y'all tryna kick it? " Tia
spoke for the both of them. "Yeah we want to slide
thru." Tia was holding her baby weight perfectly.
She just appeared to be thicker.Tia and Tiffany
stepped into the condo next to hers. They noticed
about ten white females and six black men.

The brown skin man approached them. He started the introductions. " Whats good with y'all? What's y'all names? I'm Tia and this Tiffany. Y'all fine as fuck I'm Charlie Way." Tiffany wasn't use to all the street names "Did your mama name you that? No my mother named me Charles, but you can always find your way with Charlie Way." Tia knew by the statement that Charles was indeed a pimp. She secretly missed her days of hoen. Even though it was her downfall, she may had got raped. However she loved the attention she received from pimps and tricks. She like the lifestyle of making fast money. As the night progressed; Tia noticed Tiffany was more interested In the snow bunny's. Tia thought "Is this bitch on pussy?" She didn't care enough to ask. She was busy smoking weed with Charlie Way. " So Tia you claim you was just getting money in the A. Who was you folks out there be honest? Or is you a renegade? That doesn't matter, he isn't my folks anymore. You wasn't hustling on a solo basis was you? Or did you get down with other bitches? I was a part of a small stable. That's whats up Tia I got two hoes I need a team player. They don't like drama or bullshit. Charlie where are you from? Los Angeles I've seen it all done it all, sent bitches, sold dope,robbed, killed, I've done it all baby. " Charlie Way was considered well rounded in the

269

streets. He was known as a jack of all trades. His government name was Demarcus Johnson. He had lied to both Tia and Tiffany. He got the handle Charlie Way from his obsession with. The E-40 album "Charlie hustle". He was not from California. He was from Phoenix Arizona. He was a con artist. He never told his real name or age. He was 33 he looked 19 and said he was 24. He traveled to many states. Conning young women to hoe for him. Unlike Madrix he didn't travel with hoes. Each city he went to was like a vacation to him. He felt like any bitch in the game knew her own city better then he ever could. He pimped every female he came across in their own backyard. Charlie had met the occupants of the kick back at a nearby bar. He saw the young white girls Instantly seeing dollar signs. The niggas that partied with them. Had followed Charlie and the snow bunnies . With the very same motives as Charlie. He knew the game had must gotten to Tia. She had a beautiful shape but he noticed a small pudge. She was young , pregnant fresh In the game. Tia told Charlie about her background. "So your brother is a blood and your dad is a crip wow? Damn y'all still banging colors out here wow." Tia quickly thought Charlie Way was intelligent by the way he spoke. He was fine as hell to her. 5'11, with a brown skin complexion, his hair was in a low cut ceaser, with chiseled features. Dressed In a all black Casual Gucci outfit. A black snap back hugged his head, the black button up and jeans fit him perfectly. In the middle of Tia and Charlie Ways conversation a altercation broke out. Tia saw Tobbie holding one of the young men In the condo at gun point. "Tobbie what the fuck are you doing? I came back over here to check up on y'all. I heard the loud ass music coming from over here. I assumed your raspy ass was over here. But u on some sucka shit kicking It with these G.D niggas." Tia didn't know the man Tobbie pointed the gun at. Rayshawn was a member of the G.D folks. He owed Martron five kilos of cocaine. He had gotten the drugs on consignment. Not paying his tab for over three months. Tobbie wasn't giving Rayshawn any room for more error. He pulled the trigger, the single bullet went right Inside of Rayshawn's skull. Brain matter sprayed out on to Tobbie he did not care. He had did his duty, to his big hommie and Boss by taking Rayshawns life. The helpless white chicks screamed along with Tiffany. Tobbie was ready to kill them all. "Okay blood who's house is this? Answer me before I kill all of y'all! One of the women spoke up. "Joanne please tell him." A trembling blonde started to talk. " Hi I am Joanne please don't hurt me. Please don't hurt my friends either. Tobbie put the smoking gun in Joannes hands. "What just happened was a robbery. This nigga came into your crib and tried to rob you. The two of you tussled with the gun and you shot him." The men that were there had fled while Tobbie coached a terrified Joanne. " Your finger prints are all of this gun. As you can see I have on gloves. You and your friends can report me to the police but you have no evidence. I know where you live. I can easily find out where they live. And murder every last one of you and your families." Tobbie motto was no witness no case. He didn't want to further trouble for him. By killing everyone in the house. Instead he pumped fear in them. That they would all die at his hands if they told what really happened. Tobbie handed Joanne her house phone. " Call the police, tell them somebody broke in and tried to rob you. The rest of you bitches go home. Parties over! After giving out instructions Tobbie left.

Chapter 11

" Age Ain't Nothing But A Number" by Pretty Ricky thumped our of the speakers. At the low key apartment , Tia, Charlie and Tiffany sat in. The song was perfect for the set up of a grown man hanging with teen age girls. They all conversed in the living room of the ran down apartment. It was a dump to be polite. Charlie had said the home belonged to him. Which was also fictional. The

apartment belonged to a snow bunny he dealt with

when he came into town. A cheap blow up bed and

lawn chairs were the furniture. The walls were

covered In yellowish stains, from cigarette smoke.

The low class apartment was located in North

Portland. Tucked in the back streets near beautiful

houses. It was surely misplaced. Tiffany wanted to

go home. The night was far to much for her. Tia

wanted to be around Charlie Way. Once they had

left the condo.Tiffany suggested they go home.

Until Tia saw Charlie sitting inside his car. He

invited them to "his house" to hang out and relax.

After experiencing a crazy night he knew the two

girls were afraid and vulnerable. Charlie spoke with much authority. Tia felt he was nothing like Madrix.He seemed intelligent, more then sure about himself. Charlie has a drug problem, his drug of choice was cocaine. He pulled out a baggie containing the drug. Breaking down three lines for himself and the girls. Tiffany didn't smoke weed. Trying coke would be be jumping head first into experiencing drug use. She wanted to try the drug, her reasoning was to see what all the fuss was about. Tia quickly snorted her line. Charlie Way followed suit. They danced wildly to the music coming from the used boom box. Tia straddled him, after barely knowing him for a few hours.

Tiffany tried the cocaine. It made her feel like she could not control herself she felt stuck. She did not like the feeling. Hearing the way Tia and Charlie spoke to each other. She knew what type of lifestyle Tia was living . "Tia your so damn fine I bet you could make me a rich. You would kill em beautiful. I could for sure do that. I made a killing in every state I touched. I bet your thick, chocolate ass did. I for sure did! Well let me try it out if it's that good. Aye Tiffany is your sexy ass tryna join." Tiffany was a In the closet lesbian. She was also turned off by the pimp and the conversation. Tiffany thought Tia was lame for saling ass. D-Loc was right all along with his speculations. Tiffany wanted to go home. She didn't want to bust Tia out. There was just no point of her staying the night with Tia and a man that she felt was a pervert. She noticed Tia and Charlie getting ass hole naked directly in front of her. Having enough. She put on her Purple Nike Boomer coat and her matching Nike snow boots. Leaving out of the door of the apartment .Tiffany sat at a lonesome bus stop; calling a cab. It took thirty minutes for the cab to arrive and take her across town. The cab fare was $86 dollars Tiffany didn't mind. D-Loc gave her a hefty allowance. She paid the fare. Creeping into the mansion. She made it to her room crawling in her bed. Tiffany didn't crave the

cocaine. She wondered how much she could make
If she had the chance to sale it.

 Tia sexed Charlie in every position. She was right
he was nothing like Madrix. He was ten times
worst. He had enemies in nearly every state. He
would put Tias life on the line quickly. Over money
or fear. He didn't care about anybody, not even
himself. Tia had once again fell for the gift of gab.
She was back in the trance of the pimp game.
Charlie woke Tia up explaining he had to go get
his hoe from the track. Tia was surprised he had a
women working for him that was willing to walk
82nd. A hoe stroll that had a bad reputation in
Portland. Charlie asked Tia to go with him. She

280

didn't object. They made it to 82nd and Sandy where the very young white women got Inside the car. She handed Charlie over one thousand dollars. Tia was a Portland native she was surprised, the women made that amount of money. The 82nd hoe stroll was considered low budget.Yet the young women had made a reasonable amount of money.

Martron was angry as he signed himself out of The hospital. Tobbie had phoned him, an hour after he murdered Rayshawn. Once Tobbie reiterated what took place. He knew his sister was into some heavy shit. He also worried about Tiffany. The two hadn't met. Martron was just worried about the young girl. He also had a sister.

He didn't want any teenage girl in harms way.

Tobbie described the nigga Tia was speaking to.

Martron couldn't seem to match a face with a

name. Tobbie picked Martron up, he was weak. He

wasn't going to leave his little sister out in the

dangerous streets. As he did for the past months.

He had failed Tia in a major way. She had went

from a straight A student, to a pregnant high

school drop out. He couldn't see the reality that

she was also a prostitute. Switching from Pimp to

Pimp. When Tobbie arrived he helped his friend

into his Green Camaro. Martrons weight was on his

crutches. He was hurting badly. He sucked up the

pain getting into his car. " Tobbie take me to my dads." Tobbie was caught off guard. D-Loc was a brand In his eyes regardless of him being Martrons father. Hood politics still stood tall. He had love for Martron so he would respect his wishes.

Tobbie turned the old school record "Piru love" down. " Yo you sure your pops won't be tripping? Nah blood I got you. You're a boss in the making Tobbie. I can't put your life on the line. Why did you murk Rayshawn in front of all those witnesses? I had to nigga. You told me to lay him the fuck down on sight so I did it. Don't worry the bitches there are to scared of their own fate to tell the truth. I don't know about the niggas. But the white girls that were there are spooked for sure. I'm just confused on why my sister and my dads bitches lil sister was there?" By the time Tobbie car pulled up to D-Loc's house. The sun was rising. Martron stepped outside of the car assisted by Tobbie. Martron knocked on the door for some time. He rang the doorbell back to back. D-Loc finally answered the door with sleep in his eyes. A Royal Blue silk Rob was wrapped around his naked body. " Martron why you knocking on my motherfucking door like the police? Dad It's about Tia! Boy bring you're ass on in here, you to Tobbie. D- Loc was heated being awoke from his sleep. After hitting Aujaniques pussy all night.

Martron and Tobbie stepped into Dlocs large

kitchen. That was covered in Marble counter tops,

stainless steel and chrome appliances. D-Loc

started to brew some coffee. His only son talked to

him in a sorrowful tone. "Man I need to get a hold

of Tia. Tobbie murked the G. D nigga Rayshawn."

D-Loc was disappointed hearing the news. He had

taken a liking to Rayshawn. They had been

around each other a few times In passing. "Why

did you kill him Tobbie." Before he was able to

respond Martron interjected, heading irritation In

his fathers voice. " he layed that nigga down

because I told him to. The nigga owed me five

kilos that he ran off with months ago. That's

beside the point Tia and Tiffany where there.

Where did this go down at? Next door to the condo

Tia was staying in The Pearl. Ive been calling Tia

since I left the hospital. But I don't know where

she is? She won't pick up the phone! I don't have

Tiffanys phone number. Let me call her real quick

son." D-Loc grabbed his land line phone calling

Tiffany. Her bedroom was the one lonesome room

on the main floor. The men heard her Ciara

"Goodies" ring tone blare from her phone.

Waking her up out of a deep sleep. D-Loc told

Tiffany to come Into the kitchen. He was in

Investigation mode. "Tiffany my son Martron Is

here. Because you and Tia saw some shit y'all

shouldn't had saw. What are you talking about Darren? Look Tiffany Tobbie told my son what happened. I ain't see shit!" Martron Instantly liked Tiffany's gangstah. D-Loc continued to question Tiffany. "Where in the fuck is Tia? I don't know! Yes you do! Where is the last place you saw my daughter?" Martron knew his sister had been talking to a random nigga. Martron was losing his patience. " Look Tiffany, I know you don't know me from a can of paint, but where did you last see my goddamn sister? I don't even know exactly where we was. But we were with some nigga that seemed like he was a pimp. He said his name was Charles, but he goes by Charlie Way." Tiffany didn't want to bust Tia out. She felt she was doing the right thing. They were her new family. From the way she saw Charlie Way behave. She knew he was no good. Tiffany told the truth out of worry and concern for Tia.

Chapter 12

It had been a full week since any one had spotted Tia. She was trapping out of motel rooms. Afraid that either one of her father or brothers cohorts would see her. She posted on Craigslist In the escorts category. Charlie Way sexed her good , told her false war stories. While Tia sold her body to pay his pockets. Tia didn't realize how much of an uproar her family was in. She was nearing her fifth month of pregnancy. Missing; addicted to cocaine and ecastsy. Tia didn't even take time to go to most of her doctors appointments. She did go to one single appointment where she found out she would be having a son.

She started to feel the small baby kick. Ignoring it doing more cocaine. Tia dressed in a black leather cat suit. Shaking her ass off of Beyoncé's "Crazy In Love". Looking in the mirror she just knew she was a bad bitch. Charlie watched her thinking about. How he would break her pockets, use her until he couldn't use her anymore. And toss her out on the streets like he had done to so many others. Charlie didn't stay in one place for more then 90 days. He packed up leaving women for dead. Traveling to new cities. Lying and ruining lives. Tia missed her brother, she also felt he had too much street drama.She wondered what happened to Tiffany the night they met Charlie Way, she didn't sweat it. Tia also thought about Madrix, Cynthia, and Kevin. When she did she just consumed more cocaine.

Madrix arrived in Portland on the second week of June 2005. He was 200 hundred thousand dollars richer, from his pimping trip. He was a hustler he had a stable of three bitches. They had no days off. They had better clocked him major doe. Madrix had spoken to Martron a few days after he returned home. He knew Tia was missing. At least it wasn't on his account. Martron had told him exactly what Tobbie and Tiffany told him. He knew Tia had chose up with another pimp.That was good news to his ears . He didn't want to help out with any more kids. Madrix dressed for his best friends birthday party. D-Loc was hosting Martron a 27th birthday party at the New Copper Penny night club. Madrix dressed in a throw back Blazers Jersey, black Encye jeans topping his outfit off with black Timberland boots. Martron was happy his father hadn't disrespected him inviting his enemies to his own birthday party. There were a few Hoover's in the building. Martron didn't sweat the beef. He didn't have a direct problem with the niggas. He had a Issue with David. Madrix showed up in the V.I.P section, greeting Martron the two friends embraced with a brotherly hug. " Happy bday my nigga, thanks blood. Man you looking good hommie. You up out that hospital like you never got hit. Nigga I'm a Hitta, how could I ever stay down for long!" The two men laughed. Drinking shots of Hennessy out of the bottle. Martron was clad, his fresh fade hair cut was tapered perfectly. He sported black diamonds in his ear, A black silk Georgio Armani Suit. Around his neck a customized chain read "MarRu" In yellow diamonds. His out fit was finished by black

Stacey Adams. D-Loc had been socializing with Aujanique and her coworkers that she had invited. It took him an hour to notice Madrix presence.

He approached him with hate in his heart. "What the fuck your slob ass doing here? It's my bro bday nigga what you mean blood? Aye you little slob ass bitch you need to leave before I murder your sucka ass. Only reason you catching a break is because it's too many witnesses Cuz." Madrix attempted to punch D-Loc in the face. Martron tried to stop the entire fight from happening to no avail. D-Loc drew his pistol from his waist. Shooting Madrix in his leg. Madrix stood strong, not realizing he was shot. He drew his 40.

Caliber gun. He started to recklessly shoot. All of the club attendees were terrified.Crowds ran towards the clubs exits. Madrix fled the scene. When the smoke cleared. Aujanique layed on the ground shot in her stomach three times. D-Loc tried to remain calm "Baby stay calm." He couldn't understand where he had been when she had gotten shot. He had never noticed she was standing directly next to him. " Darren I'm going to be okay. You will baby you will be okay." Martron ran to his father and Aujanique. He was instantly heart broken seeing all the blood flow out of Aujanique on to the ground. " Martron call the ambulance son! As the words left D-Loc mouth.

Aujaniques body went limp in his arms. He held her hand as she took her last breath. The events afterwards were a blur. The flashing of red and blue lights played over in D-Locs head.

Tia saw the story of Aujaniques death on the news. When she was identified as the victim. Tia shed a tear. Aujanique was a mother of two, the sole provider of her younger sister. Tia was tired of the murdering streets of Portland. She had suggested traveling with Charlie Way. He told her traveling wasn't a option. He would soon be leaving Tia and Portland behind for a while. He would take his 90 day run elsewhere. Days after Aujaniques death Tia thought about Tiffany . It had to be difficult to lose a sibling. Tia couldn't imagine losing Martron, she feared his death often because of the lifestyle he lived. On a 65 degree June night. Tia put on a casual white V neck T-shirt and blue jeans. Tias baby bump was starting to show. It made her worry she wouldn't make any more money. Charlie assured her that she would make more money. With creeps that craved pregnant women. Charlie Way told Tia his theory of why hoes who offered fetish services could make more money. There was nothing unique about a pregnant hoe. Charlie manipulated Tia by calling her pregnancy the " wonder baby". The snow bunny Charlie had was a hoe that offered

G.F.E (girlfriend experience) she treated tricks like her boyfriend she kissed, layed flat on her back in the missionary position, she held hands. She had unprotected sex with some tricks. Barebacking the men becausee she was H.I.V postive.She did not care about her health or there's. The snow bunny would do anything for the dollar.Tia was at the Motel 6 on 91st and Glisan. Her and Charlie were staying at the Airport Marriott Hotel. Tia rented rooms at the Motel 6 to hit licks. Charlie Way wanted to save money. He suggested they stay live at the Snow bunny's shaggy apartment. Tia talked him out of it by explaining. The last place Tiffany saw them was at the apartment. Tia did not want her Dad or brother showing up to the residence.

Charlie Way suggested she rent a motel room on

82nd Ave. Tia objected to hosting her dates in such

a tacky environment. Tia applied the final touches

to her makeup.Snorted a line of cocaine, got into

the rental car Charlie Way had gotten her. She

parked in the backstreet near 82nd and Flavel. Tia

walked to the Main Street. Sashaying with her new

Aline Bob hair cut. Tia wanted to change her

Image, she had always had long hair, she had

started wearing Long weaves when she dealt with

Madrix. she also wore short wigs from time to time

to disguise herself. The first date of her night

pulled up in a grey pick up truck. A Mexican man

occupied the vehicle. Tia got inside the truck , making sure to screen him to see if he was a police officer or not. Madrix had schooled her on screening. " Hey there Mija where do you want to go?" Tia sat silent until the man grabbed her left breast. He exposed his small penis. Letting her know he was indeed a John and not the police. "We can go wherever baby Its on you. Would you like to go to my room? Or would you like a car date? " Tia used a soft tone when she asked the trick what he wanted to do. "Mija I just want a quick blow job. I'm on my way to a party." The man pulled into a rocky alley. Tia pulled out a condom as the man pulled down his pants. She

299

placed It on his three inch penis. Going to work. Sucking a slurping for two minutes until the man climaxed .Tia had made 200 dollars in two minutes. It was what she craved ,the power of a quick come up. The man loved his short time with Tia,he invited her to the party he was headed to. Tia didn't want to enter a dangerous environment. Attending a party alone. Could lead to her being raped , beaten, or even killed. She Invited the man to her motel room. He was on a time schedule but he agreed to go to the motel with her for more time. Tia gave the man a massage. She then undressed taking off all of her clothes. She put another condom on and straddled the man. He climaxed within three minutes. Tia was paid $500.

She had made "easy money" in her eyes for less

then an hour. She had the trick take her to a back

street, near 82nd. She only walked for ten

minutes, when the next car pulled up. A slim white

man in a Toyota Camry was the driver. " Do you

need a ride sweetheart.". Tia thought it was so

funny how all the Johns spoke the same language

when it came to pussy. The white man quickly

exposed himself once Tia was in the car. He felt

her up. Taking the option to got to her motel

room. He was more thorough with questioning

then her last trick. He was a middle aged white

man. He wanted to know Tias age, how old she

was,how far in her pregnancy she was? He saw the baby bump and became interested. He wasn't going to cancel the date. But he did want to know who he was hanging out with. Tia had told him all lies. Including that she had a tumor in her stomach. He payed Tia $950 for a hour and a half of her time. She made over $1600 she was overjoyed with the power of her pussy and finesse. Tia had the trick drop her off to the rental car. She came back to the motel where she showered. She dressed in a valor sweat suit, putting her hair in a messy bun. She looked like the 16 year old kid she was for once. Tia stepped in the mirror taking pictures of her stomach. She wanted to talk to

Cynthia badly so she sat down and wrote her a letter.

Chapter 13

" Dear Cynthia,

Hey girlie, I know you haven't heard from me in forever. I miss you so fucking much. I don't know if Martron told you, but bitch I'm pregnant. I just found out Im having a son. I'm five months. Please don't be mad at me but I dropped out and I got my G.E.D. There's so much I need to tell you. My life is so crazy. I need to get down there to see you. I need a visiting application ASAP. How is It going in there? Are you on pussy yet? Girl tell me the truth! You're my best friend, I feel so closed in. There's so much going on with me. I haven't even told Martron the truth. And you better not tell him what I'm about to tell you. I told my family Kevin is my baby's daddy. But I know my baby is by Madrix! I dissed Kevin at my party. Plus I've been doing shit you will think is foul. I can't explain It on paper. You will understand In person. Well I'm going to wrap this letter up. Love you. My birthday is May 15th in case you can fill out the form for me. Well your my bestie you know when my birthday is.

P.S Make sure you shoot me a form so I can come to see you."

Tia had acquired a P.O. Box, specifically for Cynthia to be able to reach her. Tia sat on the motel weeping. She was a fuck up, a powder head, a hoe, everyone around her was getting hurt, taken away, or dying. As she shed tears Charlie Way called her. "What's good Tia?, nothing." Charlie could hear Tia crying. He didn't like handling anyone's emotions not even his own. "Are you done working? Yes. Cool I can come get you and we can go to the Hotel and crash for the night.Charlie drove drunk off a pint of Hennessy. He knew pregnant women were emotional with all of their hormones. He knew Tia was depressed. He expected the worst from her emotionally. The poor girl had been robbed and raped. Charlie Way was a pimp so it was his duty, to play the role of a caring human being. He didn't care about Tia's well-being he was in character. His only concern was his money. Once they made it to the hotel room. Charlie sat her on his lap. "Tia are you okay baby? No..." she whimpered. He rocked her back in forth. While her tears dropped down his right shoulder. He picked Tia up carrying her to the king size bed. Pulling her pants down. Diving right into her pussy with his tongue. He was boyfriend pimping. Doing sexual acts that no pimp should do with a hoe. Misleading her for his own gain. He knew the head he gave her would make her relax easing up. To get inside her head. Pimps have fucked their hoes since the beginning of pimping.

There were to be certain rules in the game. Charlie was not following the rule of protected sex and no oral sex, meeting parents, doing family outings, and love making was all considered simp (sucka, Imitating,a,pimp) shit.

Once Tia came all over Charlie Ways face. She gave him $900 he was satisfied . She had learned from Mahogany. Except she didn't put her money Into an account. She hid it In her makeup bag. Charlie never purse checked her, he surely wouldn't go thru her makeup bag. Tia's fear wasn't Charlie finding out she was tucking money from him. Her fear was running into D-Loc or Martron. She had a gut feeling that Tiffany had spilled the beans about her and Charlie way. She

knew her father or brother would not hesitate to

put a bullet in his head. They would do damage to

anyone who threatened her wellbeing. The

narcotics mad her less conscious of her decisions.

Causing her not to prepare for the birth of her son.

Tia did not worry about her own health. She

consumed liquor and drugs like it was going out of

style.

  Tia sat gazing at Charlie, while he broke down

four lines of cocaine. On the small table that was

in their hotel room.Charlie Way had a way to

make her feel like her problems didn't exist. "Tia I

swear on my mama you be hitting, thank you. You

make so much money you make a nigga want to wife you. Really? Why are you questioning me? Because before you I was told there's no love in this game. The nigga you fucked with before me was right when it comes to a cum bucket bitch. But who wouldn't love your chocolate ass?I don't know about all that. Well I love you. Wow I love you too. But look at me baby I'm all pregnant and shit. You can't really want me. That baby is a gift from above. Imma love that baby as much as I love you I promise. When you have the baby Im going to take you to Cali to meet my people. You can take care of the baby for a while then go back to work. I'll watch him." The conversation paused while they both snorted the cocaine. Charlie Way lied to Tias face. He didn't care about her or her unborn child. He would flee to a different state. Perhaps the east coast. He had killed countless men. Yet seeing the way Tobbie killed Rayshawn. He knew Martron or D-Loc weren't the niggas to play with. He couldn't take the chance with his life. He was a daredevil, loving to test the limits. Testing whether he would get caught slipping by Portland gangsters was not his forte'.

He did live everyday like it was his last, fucking people over every chance he got. Caused him to be paranoid.

D-Loc sat in his living room devastated. He was vexed Aujanique had not been dead a full week. He was full of regret and sorrow. He told the twins and Tiffany he couldn't hold it together. He didn't shower, eat,or sleep. He drank and drank. The twins felt sorry for him. Tiffany didn't, she was older,she blamed him for her sister death. The home was often times quiet. The twins dad Victor live in Houston Texas. He was expected to come to Portland for Aujaniques funeral. Victor was a deadbeat dad. The twins were 13, he hadn't saw them since they were two years old. He lived in Houston with his wife and three children. He was active in his other kids life. He had married a white women. Wanting nothing to do with his black kids. Victor was a sale out! He was 15 years older then Aujanique. When she became pregnant with his twin sons he left her for dead.He saw his children three times up until they were the age two. Disappearing from their life completely, shortly after.Victor was to take over the responsibilities of his children, now that his baby's mother was deceased. He was saddened that he would have to come retrieve full black children. There were plenty of people who had biracial children, who had not turned their backs on their own race. Victor was not one of those people

Tiffany was headed to foster care. The closet relative she had was an Aunt in New York that she had never met. No one could reach the aunt. Tiffany would become a ward of the state. D-Loc did not want the twins with Victor, or Tiffany in states custody. However there weren't any other options. A DHS worker had come to D-Locs house. Informing him that there was no way he could possibly get the children legally. The state of Oregon was doing their best to split the twins up from Tiffany. Saying it was in their best interest. He worried more about Tiffany then the twins. He did think victor was a sucka. But the foster care system was not where he felt a child belonged.

Especially a 16 year old girl. Who had never been in the system before. D-Loc sat In his living room. Dressed in a cream Yves Saint Laurent outfit, with comfy house shoes waiting for the funeral planner to arrive. When the dorky funeral home director rang the door bell. D-Loc opened his front door, looking as if he was 65 years old. He had aged drastically due to the lost of his queen. He had encountered the man twice before. He quickly let him in. " Hey there Darren thank you for inviting me to your home. No problem, I didn't feel like driving. What a lovely hime you have.Thanks, Well I've decided I want the grey marble head stone. Okay sir I'm going to write that down. Also I hired my own makeup artist. I don't want her not looking like herself and shit. Sir we have great artist. I don't care it's already paid for. We scheduled the viewing of the body for 5pm. The funeral planner and D-Loc spoke for another thirty minutes. Everything was planned to the tee, when Dloc showed him out of his home. Aujanique funeral would be nice, on behalf of D-Loc. He invested in sending her home properly. The twins were in the kitchen whispering. D-Loc walked into the area in his home in a questionable manner. D-Loc inquires on their conversation. " What y'all In here talking about?" Deshawn spoke up. "We don't wanna go with our fucking dad man". The

315

young mans gangster was coming out now that his mother was no longer with them. "Deshawn that's your father, if I keep y'all here it will be considered kidnap. Treyshawn began to cry he couldn't take any more pain " Man Darren please let us stay. We aren't mad at you man. We know it's not your fault please don't make us go with our dad." Treyshawn wrapped his arms around D-Loc in a warm embrace. Bringing tears to the grown mans face. He had grown to love the twins. Unlike the boys he did blame himself for Aujaniques death. Had he never argued with Madrix. She would had never died. D-Loc was only trying to protect his daughter. By trying to be a father to Tia he lost the love of his life. Deep In his thoughts he was caught off guard by his doorbell ringing. He looked thru his peep hole seeing it was his son. He knew Martron was not there for small talk. Martron stepped in the foyer wearing a red tall tee. Red monkey jeans and red, black and white Jordan 13's. He was flamed up, that was his style, daily attire. The father and son hadn't saw each other since the shooting. Martron didn't personally want to kill Madrix. He did feel that street justice needed to be served. He was tired of innocent people losing their lives. Aujanique was a grown women. That had never been in any street drama. Dloc was no longer an active gang member. Nobody could understand how her death came about. No one knew it was personal vs. street. " Where you think that bitch ass nigga at son? Who knows you know Madrix stay moving around. Yes I know. He will be touched, I still got crip homeboys all across the country. That will fo' sho' kill a weak ass nigga for me. The nigga gonna get bodied where he stand. Dad have you heard from Tia? Martron and D-Loc had both been in North Portland looking for Tia. Tiffany had stated they had last hung out in the North side of Portland. Martron planned on finding his sister. He wanted to kill the out of towner badly. He wanted to show him Portland niggas were not to be tested.

" No son I haven't been able to get in touch with her. Well keep me on the up and up if you do talk to her.

Tia was once again preparing to walk the track. She sat in the motel 6 room drinking Grey Goose. Doing her drug of choice cocaine. It had been a complete week since Aujaniques death. Witnesses described the killer. As a black man in his mid 20's with light skin, tall and slender. Tia knew in her heart of hearts It was Madrix. She knew her reckless behavior had caused the sweet women to loose her life. Tia put down the alcohol and cocaine. She had been sitting in the motel room naked. After taking a steamy shower. She lotioned her body with bath and body works. Japanese Cherry blossom lotion. Tia did not feel like doing her hair. She slicked her hair into a messy bun with brown pro style hair gel. Charlie Way no longer rented the car for Tia. She called a Radio cab. The cabbie seemed to be interested in giving her more then a ride. Which didn't bother her. She was a hustler, always wanting time make some money. Tia rode in the cab not realizing there was no rear view mirror. The cabbie spoke to her aggressively. " Hey there baby do you offer blow jobs? I usually see your hot ass strolling up and down 82nd." The cabbie was a middle age Italian man. Tia didn't think to screen him because he was a cab driver. Tia exposed her breast to the

man. As quickly as she exposed herself was as

quickly as the cab pulled over. Two cop cars

swarmed the cab. The cab driver was an

undercover cop. The Portland police had come up

with the Idea to use cabs as a way to do stings on

local prostitutes. Tia felt defeated as she was

handcuffed and placed in the back of the patrol

car. Upon discovering her real identity the police

had to transfer Tia from the adult facility Inverness

to the youth facility JDH. She was placed in the

youth jail on 68th and Halsey. Tia felt stupid In her

6x9 jail cell. She would not give up any

information on any relatives. She was miserable as

she sat in jail for two days. Having only a small comb, cheap tooth paste and and deodorant. She was angry, accustomed to having the best materials. She lay miserable In her cell on the thin mattress. When she heard music to her ears. "Brandt roll up, you're aunt is here to get you." Tia didn't know what aunt had come to get her. Her aintie lived in Texas. As she entered the lobby of JDH. A petite Hispanic officer walked up to her. Handing her a slip of paper. "Ms. Brandt your court date is on June 28th, you will most likely be assigned a juvenile court counselor. Since you have no prior criminal history and the charge your facing is a misdemeanor. Tia never gave the petite

Officer any conversation. She was escorted to her "aunt". A chunky black women wearing a church hat. Tia had never saw the women a day in her life. The women hugged Tia, speaking loudly causing a scene. " Hey baby what were you doing out so late? They talking about some prostitution madness with my baby." The women rocked Tia back and forth. Tia had no idea what was going on, she played Into the role of knowing the women because she wanted to get out of jail. Once they made it outside of the juvenile detention center. The women led Tia to a burgundy Buick century. Charlie Ways snow bunny was in the passenger seat. Tia went on and on regarding the worst two days of her life. " Girl you don't know what I had to go thru in there. The shit was terrible. Nasty food,a small ass tv,in the day room. That I barley got to go In. A raggedy ass bed; I couldn't wait to get the fuck out of that place. It sucks, I never want to go back. Well Charlie paid this lady to forge some papers and come with a fake birth certificate to get you out. So just be happy your out." The snow bunny spoke with a hard tone. She didn't care for Tia. The young girl was stealing her shine. She didn't like what was going on with Tia and Charlie Way.

Chapter 14

Aujaniques funeral service was packed to capacity. Her coworkers, friends and some of her former patients all attended the service. For D-Loc the event was déjà vu. He had already buried both of his baby's mothers. Aujanique laid in a gold casket. Her hair was pinned Into a beautiful French roll. Beautiful neat curls were formed around her face cascading from the Updo She wore a cream Vera wang sequence gown. Her skin glowed as It had when she was alive. The make up artist was worth paying. Aujanique looked like she was only asleep. A sleeping beauty. Photos of her were blown up poster size. Sitting on tripods.

There were pictures of her at work, pictures of her alone the most heart wrenching photos were of Aujanique and her sons. The photos with her and Tiffany were just as hurtful. Dloc walked to the pull pit during the service to speak. Anticipating the dirty looks he would get from the patrons. He spoke into the microphone. " Good morning my name is Darren. The women laying here before us. Is the only women I ever had any respect for. Aujanique commanded attention when she walked into any room. When I met her I knew I would eventually ask her to be my wife. I accepted her children and sister as my own. Every moment with them has been amazing. Life didn't last long for this beautiful angel. She changed who I was and showed me how to become a man. Because of her I will never disrespect another black women. Aujanique loved all people because of her I will never disrespect another women. I will forever honor her. Everyday I wake up I feel like god should had taken my life and not hers." D-Loc whimpered stepping down from the pull pit. Not noticing all the funeral attendants, including his son , the twins and Tiffany all stood to their feet. The audience felt his pain. After the burial of Aujanique. D-Loc hosted a after pass at his house. The twins would be leaving with their father and he was not happy with that reality. Victor approached D-Loc. "I liked what you had to say thank you for looking out for my sons. I had no choice. I can't really talk because I haven't been the best dad to my own kids. But nigga where was you at? You left them their whole lives. The situation is complex. I was married to my wife when I got Aujanique pregnant. My wife would not accept the boys. So you picked a bitch over your kids? You telling me you left your sons because of how a bitch felt! Hold on man you don't have to come off so rude. I'm being rude nigga? You in my house playing like you give a fuck about your kids! You don't know how I feel now that I know I have to feed two growing boys. The shit is overwhelming. Martron watched the conversation from afar. He knew It was getting heated, He approached the discussion, knowing his father was hot headed. " What's good my nigga? Do you have a issue with my pops?No I don't, I was going to suggest sending the boys out here twice a year." D-Loc was irked by the deadbeat father that was in his face.

" Man take on your responsibilities. Aujanique would had never wanted them with you. Because you ain't gonna love them right. You're a Uncle Tom. Cuz you need to step your game up. You have me mistaken I want to be in my sons lives I want to know them. I assumed since they had been staying with you and like it here. They could come see you sometimes. My sons will be fine they are light like me so they will fit in. Nigga are you crazy, you're trying to say your kids will fit in because of their complexion? To say they will fit in because they high yellow with Red hair is some dumb shit. They didn't even get the hair color from you. It came from Aujaniques black mother dummy. D-Loc started to fumble with the inside of his suit jacket. The entire repast started to watch him. Including the twins and Tiffany. Victor was offended. He continue to put his foot in his mouth. " Don't you dare have comments on how I view my sons!" Before D-Loc could react Martron knocked him to the ground, with a strong hit to his jaw. D-Loc and

Martron stomped Victor out. A few of the men

attending the repast had to pull them off of Victor.

He rose from the ground with his mouth bleeding

as well as his nose. Victor got the ass whooping

that was coming to him. The twins were upset they

ran up to the altercation. "Darren please don't

make us go with this nigga please." Treyshawn

cried, the twins cried in unison. They didn't

deserve what was happening to them. They had

lost their mother. Now they were being forced to

live with a stranger that gave them life. But did

not know or love them. The twins felt defeated

when they got inside their fathers house leaving

the mansion. They felt like they would never see their hometown again.

Tiffany was numb to everything happening around her. The funeral was on a Saturday, the upcoming Monday would be the day her social worker came. Tiffany would enter the foster care system. Martron sat in his new house in Beaverton Oregon. He was preparing to meet his connect when he saw he had a incoming call from Cynthia. " Hey baby, Whats up love how are you doing? Good I'm going to church almost every day, working out just thanking god, sho' ya right baby I'm proud of you. How are you Martron? I'm okay could be much better. I haven't talked to Tia.

That's what I was going to ask you about she just wrote me. What did she say? Baby can you sit down." Martron knew if Cynthia was asking him to sit down . She was going to give him bad news. He was hoping she hadn't been in any trouble resulting in losing good time. His mind raced she did tell him she heard from Tia. Cynthia took a slow deep breath. " Tias pregnant baby, yeah I've been known that, no you don't know what I'm about to tell you. She wrote me saying her baby is by Madrix. Martron I'm worried about her. What has she been doing out there? I'll read you what she wrote, I have the letter right here. " I told my family that Kevin's my baby dad but I know my son is by Madrix." What the fuck is she talking about? Nigga obviously she has been smashing Madrix." Martron had told Cynthia what his fathers speculations were. D-Loc had been right the entire time. Martron had been played. "Cyn this is too much for me call me at your next day room." Martron hung up in Cynthias face. He called Veda inquiring about Madrix. She informed him that her baby's daddy wasn't in town. She did divulge she was home. He was going to give her an unannounced visit. He didn't have to meet his connect for two hours, that gave him enough time to pop up on Veda. He drove quickly to her house.

He rang the doorbell twice, Veda opened the door dressed skimpily in lingerie. Her beautiful pedicured toes showed. "What's up with you Martron? I told you Madrix isn't In town. Yes I know I wanted to talk to you. Oh come on In." Veda led him to the large white room no one ever sat in. She sat on the Swede white sectional couch. With her feet tucked under her butt. Making it pop out more then It usually did. Martron sat on the other end of the couch "Veda did you know Madrix was fucking my little sister? Martron I have no Idea what you're talking about. I'm always out working. That nigga cheat so much I have no clue what he does. I don't want to be in this drama

Martron." Veda was happy deep down inside.

Madrix was finally getting caught up. If he died she

would be rich. She knew all of his account

information and the code to his safe. She planned

to take over his pimp empire and retire her pussy.

" Veda be real with me. Me and you have a

friendship outside of Madrix. I know you love your

baby dad but I know you know something?Well

Tia was sleeping with him. We were all in Vegas

together getting money." Martron was angry with

himself. He had been so blind. It wouldn't be his

father that would kill Madrix. He would take care

of him himself. Veda expected Martron to spazz

out.She didn't know how strategic he truly was. He

sat in silence with a Ice grill. He spoke after three minutes of silence. " Veda thank you for telling me the truth. You know I never liked how Madrix treated you. Where is lil Madrix? He is with my mom. Veda scoot closer to me." Veda scooted right next to Martron. "Why do you fuck with a nigga who treats you like shit? He be exploiting you and shit. Because I love him I put up with his shit. I know he doesn't give a fuck about me. Martron loved how vulnerable Veda was being. She went into a deep conversation about how Madrix had turned her out to hoen. She did not think he genuinely loved their son. Her family hated Madrix and had shunned her. She wished Madrix was more like Martron. Veda was miserable and wanted out of the situation. Martron had her right where he wants her slipping in her own home. He listened to her vent for an entire hour. He began to press Veda for sex. She was not against it. She wanted to get back at Madrix and Martron was handsome to her. She led him to her plushed out bedroom. The master bedroom was 500 square feet. A 72 inch tv was mounted on the wall. A cherry red wood bed frame matched a dresser and chaise. Veda had a huge chrome vanity. The walk in closet was large one side was Madrix the other Veda. Every designer label hung in the closet. Two

Swede chair's were placed in the middle for seating.

Martron pulled a magnum condom out of his pants pocket. he pulled Vedas lingerie bottoms to the side. He mounted Veda from behind. " Throw it back baby,freak that dick baby, oh my god Martron I always wanted this." His dick pulsated her pussy as he pumped in and out. Veda was in another world. The feeling was beyond euphoric. "You like that bitch,yes daddy this dick is fire.You would do whatever for this dick huh? Yes I will! Where Is Madrix. Baby I told you I don't know. I'm nutting bitch you do got some good ass pussy. Where is he? I don't know. Okay bitch you gave me the wrong answer." Before Veda could turn around and gather her thoughts. Martron pointed a pistol to the back of her head. "Where's Madrix bitch? Martron please don't kill me I told you I don't know. Bitch you are just as guilty as he is. Y'all had my little sister out there saling pussy. You're a dirty ass bitch. What's the code to the safe? 17-26-55." Once Veda answered him he knew she was worth no more information. He shot her in the back of the head killing her execution style.

Martron found over two million dollars in the safe. He thought Madrix was smarter then that. Why would he keep that large amount of money in his house? He looked at Vedas bloody head laying face down on her bed. He couldn't wait to murder Madrix.

Chapter 15

Martron didn't feel a ounce of remorse for murdering Veda. He knew it would be a wake up call for Madrix. Martron had declared war he knew Madrix wasn't afraid to let bullets fly. What Martron didn't take Into account was Madrix low level of love for Veda. In his pimp mind she was just another hoe bitch. He was all for himself. He viewed his own son as a mistake. He didn't love Veda or the child. He didn't even love himself. He loved Instant gratification and being talked about around town for getting money. He liked having a image. Martron washed the money he hijacked from Madrix. Putting it into a offshore account. Veda was found dead in her home, by her mother, the day after Martron murdered her. He flicked thru the channels focused on business.

All the drama in his life was distracting. He hadn't met his connect. He sent Tobbie. Martron looked at the duffle bags full of 20 kilos of cocaine. He had to put the coke in the streets. He called Tobbie giving him two kilos . He called Kevin's brother Johnny giving him 4 kilos Martron knew Johnny had major moves out of state. He needed a bigger load. He distributed 3 kilos to a few Kerry crip niggas. The rest he would move on his own. Martron sold half a bird or a full bird with the licks he had. He was a hustler, he didn't care about gang shit when it came to money, he cared about the profit.

   Martron contacted his dad about a meeting at The Denny's restaurant in the Lloyd district. He wanted to discuss what Cynthia told him about Tia. He had a hour to meet his dad . He showered, shaved looking at himself In the mirror. He was the spiriting image of his father. He dressed in a burgundy Gucci velour suit. Clad in White Nike Air Force ones. He sped on the highway merging on to the Seattle north section. He got off on the broadway exit. His thoughts were on his sister Tia.

He thought about the ways she was fucking her life

up. Martron wanted Madrix head for introducing

his sister to hoen. He also wanted to learn

everything he could, about the mysterious Charlie

Way. He planned to torture the man to death.

D-Loc beat his son to the Denny's restaurant.

Sitting in the booth where he ordered, steak and

eggs. He had saw Vedas death on the news, he did

not know any details of the situation. He did feel

like it was Madrix karma for Aujaniques murder.

Martron was exactly ten minutes late, when he

stepped into the double glass doors of the hoodest

Denny's in Portland. "What's good pops? Nothing

much nigga you asked me to come here and you're ass is late. Calm down old man I'm only a few minutes late." Martron quickly ordered a grand slam meal. D-Loc asked in a whisper tone. "Did you hear about Veda?" Martron let out a evil laugh. " That's why I called you here. Pops I bodied that stank ass bitch. I'm laughing to keep from crying. You was right the whole time about Madrix. Cynthia called me, Tia wrote her a letter saying the baby is Madrix's. I put two And two together that If she's pregnant by the nigga he must had been pimping her too. Did the bitch Veda lead you to Madrix? Nah man I was fucking the bitch and all. Pointed a pistol to her head and she

345

still didn't give him up. I thought Madrix was my ace, he pimped my sister with Vedas help. The bitch had to die. Why would you fuck her? You know your DNA is gonna be inside the bitch. Nigga I'm not nasty like you I used a rubber and took it when I left. I hit they stash spot too. Dumb ass nigga had two million in his safe." D-Loc gave his son dap. He was proud that his son handled his In the streets. He always wanted Martron to take a different path, since his son decided to be a street nigga. He accepted it, knowing he wasn't a sucka and could protect himself. "What address did Tia write from? Damn dad I didn't even ask Cyn. Ask her when she call, that can help us find Tia. In the meanwhile we need to find this nigga Charlie Way. Did Tiffany ever tell you what the dude looked like? Imma call her real quick hold up." D-Loc reached Inside his coat pocket. As their food arrived he dialed Tiffany's number. She answered on the third ring. " Hey Tiffany, Hey Darren what's up? Do you remember what the nigga Charlie Way looked like. Ummmm.... he had a philly hair cut. Brown skin, he was tall, skinny, I would say handsome. D-Loc hung up with Tiffany. Dialing the hood gossip phone number Rhonda. " Hello who dis? Man girl this D-Loc, oh what's good with you baby, I got a question for you? Spit It. Do you know a cat name Charlie Way? Hell nah who In the fuck is a damn Charlie Way? What type of dumb ass name is that? Rhonda If you know him just tell me. I don't know him or of him. And nigga you never fucking paid me for the last info. I don't know no motherfuckin Charlie way bye! Rhonda hung up in the ol' gs face. D-Loc dug Into his plate eating his food with an attitude. He was upset that the nigga was pimping on his daughter. He had no access to him.

After Tias run in with the law. Charlie way decided it was best she only post ads and do outcalls. He thought 82nd Avenue was to hot for her. She could no longer walk the track. The internet would be her playground. Tia was not

348

allowed to stay at the motel 6 anymore. She sat in her hotel room at the Shilo Inn, snorting lines of cocaine. She listened to Mac Dre "Feeling like that nigga." On her portable c.d player rapping the lyrics outloud. " I'm not with the drama, so you can save the theatrical, I macked on your bitch cuz she appeared to be mackable."Tia never really listened to Mac Dre until she went on the road with Madrix. Charlie was in the shower as she rapped the record. Tia had braided her own hair in Micro single braids. Giving her hair a break from the flat iron. She was dressed in a baby phat Capri set, with baby phat Sandals. Charlie Way stepped out the shower glistening In water. The sex addicted man didn't hesitate to stick his dick down Tia's throat.She slurped as her phone started to ring. Tia stopped sucking Charlie's dick. She had a date. The lick was at a motel off interstate. Deciding she had to switch up her trap spots couldn't be In the same place for too long. So she switched from The Marriott ,to The Shilo Inn to rinky dink motels one interstate. Tia pulled up In the Cadillac Deville rental car. Tia felt eyes on her; David had spotted her. He happened to be in the area visiting one of his many baby's moms and kids. He needs gas he parked at the 76 gas station directly next to the motel Tia was staying at. Right as she opened her door two shots were fired at her. Tia immediately placed the keys in the ignition restarting the car. David ran after Tias car shooting at the windows with no results. He desperately wanted to murder her believing she had set his brother Kevin up. Tia sped to the freeway nervous with tears flowing down her face. The radio played a new hit "Run It" by a new cat named Chris Brown. Tia couldn't even bob her head to the music. He nerves were too bad. She yelled out loud to herself. "I need to get my fucking life together? I'm about to have a baby and niggas want me dead and shit. God why, why, Is my life so fucked up? Why Is everything so horrible In my life right now?" Tia was miserable, feeling once again like she had nobody. After their meeting at Denny's, Martron felt the urge to find Charlie Way. He wouldn't call around like his dad. He was going to look.

The night after the Denny's meeting Martron decided to go to The Red Sea night club located in downtown Portland. The club was packed to capacity as the Rasta music bumped Martron watched the patrons grind on each other. He wasn't interested in dancing or socializing. He had came to the club for one reason and one reason only. Martron also rode solo not interested in a codefendant in a public place. Martron sat by the bar sipping a Incredible Hulk. He then decided to use the bathroom knowing drunk ass niggas loved to talk while pissing. Martron sat In a stall as two men debated over the Trail Blazers and The Los Angeles Lakers. One of the men was a short, sloppy chocolate man, The lakers fan was a slender caramel complexed man. "Man fuck the blazers y'all hella weak, well why you in the town then, because my mama moved out here I rep the bay yadiiamean." Martron creeped out of the stall with a 9mm in his hand. While the two men argued they never noticed him he had a loaded gun In his possession. Martron walked up to the lakers fan, pointing his pistol speaking clearly. "Are you Charlie Way?hell nah partna who Charlie?" The lakers fan was scared for his life. "Wrong answer

Partna" Martron put a single bullet between the mans eyes. The blazers fan tried to leave but Martron lived y the motto"no witness, no case". Martron put two bullets Into the mans back as he tried to leave. Martron then left the club, the two murders he committed were useless he was acting on rage and not truth. Killing random people making himself hot. He was losing his mind looking for Charlie way.

"Tia get ya green eye having ass up! I'm flying out to Philly this week to see my regular, I already talked to Martron to look after ya, you better have ya fast ass at Jeff 8:00am sharp or Imma go ham on ya lil ass when I get back girl, sometimes you act just like that daddy of yours." Tia woke up in a cold sweat having a dream about Nyemiah, as usual on her mother was lecturing her about school. Although Nyemiah was a drug addicted prostitute she wanted the best for Tia deep down inside. Tia checked her watch to see what time it was. The fake Rolex she rocked read 3:00am! Tia thought to herself. "I can't get her off my mind lately mom what are you tryna tell me?" Tia looked over at Charlie knocked out in a Hennessy coma. She quickly dressed in a black towel sweat suit. She didn't even take the time to remove the pink Florissant head scarf, that she had wore to sleep the previous night. Tia crept out the room getting into a Toyota Camry rental. Driving the speed limit, restless Tia placed Destiny's Child's second album "Writing on the Wall" into the deck. Although the cd was six years old, it would always be a classic in her mind. Pulling up to her P.O. Box Tia read the time 4:30am she couldn't believe she was out and about, at the ass crack of down checking her mail. However she desperately needed Cynthia. When she placed the key in her P.O. Box she found exactly what she was looking for. A letter addressed from her best friend . Tia quickly hopped into Camry. Pulling into a vacant Target parking lot. Opening the letter was full of emotion for Tia. She missed her former life.She deeply missed Cynthia and hated she was locked

up in prison.

" Dear Tia,

What's up mama? So your Prego wow! Well what's

really going on with u? Talk to me gurl. I don't

even have you number to holla at chu. Thank you

for shooting me your info, you are approved to

visit me. Bitch all you gotta do is bring your I. D.

Don't wear no denim or no jeans at all.I work

Monday thru Friday in this stank ass kitchen here.

So I want you to come on a Saturday visits are

from 1-4 pm. Or 6-9 pm as for me I'm good

exercising and reading hella. Most of all I'm happy

to be getting closer to god. If It wasn't for him I'd

go insane in here. I see my mom a lot she stay up here, she mostly come during the week when I'm tryna get outta work. I'm in a open dorm, county was hell in a cell and shit. I like minimum I'll tell you all about it when you bring ya ass up here.

These bitches is hella tryna turn me out but I'm so in loveeeeeee with you brother. Sorry this letter so short but I tell you everything when you come."

Tia was so happy to know she was on Cynthias visiting list. By the time she arrived back at the hotel It was 5:20 am. Tia was more excited that It was indeed a Saturday. Charlie hadn't even moved since she left. Tia knew she couldn't sleep. She removed a small mirror from the in table next to the bed. Creating two small lines of cocaine. She quickly snorted the powder, she had became heavily addicted to the drug. Her main focus was what she would wear to visit Cynthia. Jeans were a no go and she didn't wanna walk in the prison In them. She looked thru three tons of clothes. Tia found a simple beige sweater dress, black leggings and four inch black over the knee Louis Vuitton boots. Tia showered leaving the hotel room at 8:00am. She put the Camry In reverse to drive out Shilo inn. Traffic wasn't heavy due to the time of morning it was the weekend. Driving with no real destination. Tia pulled over into the McDonald's parking lot located at the north end of Martin

Luther King Jr. Blvd and Columbia. She needed to kill time. Tia stepped Into the restaurant ordering three sausage and egg McMuffins two hash browns and orange juice. She got into the rental car deciding to switch out of it. In fear that she may run Into David again. Tia drove down Columbia pulling into north Portland Enterprise . The sloppy dressed man that worked the front office, tricked with Tia from time to time. He gave her the hook up on rentals knowingly giving her several rental cars, when she used fake identification. The sloppy dressed man's name tag read Sam. As Tia stepped in looking flawless In her attire, Sams dick instantly got hard ."Hey there honey what type of whip are you looking for today." Sam was trying

to sound hip using urban slang. "I want that red

Impala I saw It outside that's hot,how much Sam

baby, oh $70 a day for you. I'll give you a weekly

rate of $220 and cut you a real deal if you give me

some of your loving girl." Tia couldn't and

wouldn't turn down the deal. She quickly agreed

to the bargain stepping into the back office giving

Sam a blow job. He was a dumb easy trick, It

didn't take any finessing with him. He risked his

job security for a two minute nut. Tia didn't give a

fuck she was on her grind. Even Charlie didn't

know about the arrangement she had made. She

would make sure he didn't know. In her mind it was none of his business.

Chapter 16

Martron sat In the living room of his spot. Making a game plan, one way or another he would murder Madrix and Charlie Way. He was thinking out loud. " Who the fuck do this simp ass nigga Charlie bitch ass Way think he fucking with? I will murk that Cali nigga where he stand." Summer was approaching . Martron planned to bring in the new season with a bang. He hadn't been hanging around his hommies much but he sent word for a meeting. Martron wanted to hold the meeting. He wanted to hold the meeting at his homeboy

Lamars house. Which was around the corner from one of the blood parks Woodlawn. Martron walked to his kitchen retrieving his red razor cell phone calling Lamar on speaker phone as he prepared a B.L.T on wonder bread. " What's good nigga? what's up blood Martron you been MIA forever my nigga, I know Lamar how's everything been lookin, pretty boo the crab niggas been on bullshit as usual. But they funking with each other let them dummies kill each other. Who trippen? The snooves and them sissy niggas fonking. Oh well that's none of my concern. I got business with niggas from both of they hoods. As long as I get my money I don't give a fuck. Them niggas getting money eating just like we is. I can't worry about they politics It ain't none of our business. Well let's hold a hood meeting at your house tonight. Aight my mom will be here for sure."Lamars mom was Casey Smith a original Fruit town Piru from California. The women was 39, a teenage mother is what she had been to Lamar. She was known as Mama Blood. She provided her sons homeboys with shelter, food, stored money, drugs and supplied guns to the bloods. She had laid a few niggas down In her lifetime. Casey wasn't the only women that made the moves she made. Their were women like her in every hood from the crips to the Hoover's, holding their hoods down. Products of their environments. "That's cool I knew your mom

would be there. I can't wait to see her. Imma let

everybody know we having a meeting at 8 a clock.

Aight see you then bro." Martron ate his sandwich

lighting a blunt, looking at his Rolex watch. The

time read 2:00pm. He needed to kill time. He

showered got dressed in a black adidas hoodie,

black dickies and black Adidas shell toe shoes.

Martron was completely dressed by 3:30pm. He got

inside his white Range Rover. He drove from his

Beaverton home m to Geneva's Hair salon on N.E

MLK BlVd. He arrived at 4:25 pm, traffic was stuck

during the late afternoon.

When Martron stepped into the hair salon his barbers chair was empty. His barber was a square cat he grew up with named Ray Ray. The two men shook hands. " What's up Martron, I haven't saw you In a minute.Nothing much my nigga just living. I'm glad you recovered, we was praying for you here at the shop. You been growing your hair out or something? Nah I just wanted a philly, that's different from your usual waves but I got you nigga." Martron sat in the chair as all the females in the shop gawked at him like they were kids In a candy store. He was not interested in any of the women. His mind was on his money and Murder. When Martron had a mission to complete. He stuck to his goals, putting pussy to the side. Having learned years ago how dangerous it was to think with his dick. It could get him killed, Martron did not have time for that type of smoke.

Ray Ray knew he was in Killer mode, knowing Martron for years he didn't even bother questioning him. Ray Ray just wanted his money, he didn't gossip about anything that didn't apply to him making his bread. After he finished cutting Martrons hair he turned him towards the mirror. " You like it my nigga? I do I like it a lot, it's dope looks good on you." Martron handed Ray Ray a stiff one hundred dollar bill. He respected the mans hustle, always tipping him handsomely. He envied his barber. He had avoided the drama in the streets. Having a family, putting his three children and his wife first. Martron left the shop driving to a corner store on 18th and Dekum. He bought a swisher sweet, broke his weed down into small pieces rolling a thick blunt. He made his daily call to his baby's mother Monica to check in on her and his daughter Marshaylee was his eldest child he had met Monica when he was 16 years old. He was transporting coke to Oakland California.Monica was a drug mule at the time a runner. She was a slim, tall chocolate beauty. She had slanted eyes, full lips and a button nose. She wore her hair in a Hair cut like Nia Long. Her drive and ambition turned Martron on. He got her pregnant on one of his trips to her hometown. He didn't regret having his daughter Marshaylee. However Monica was difficult to deal with. She was a D-Girl. She wasn't comfortable with being a stay at home mom. When Martron met Zayley he knew he could build with her more. She was naturally submissive. Meeting Zayley caused him to love Monica less. She played her position well. Some men could deal with independent females others preferred those they could control. Monica was not a hood rat she didn't put up with any bullshit. She remained loyal to Martron although he started another family. She was not the type of person to wear her feeling son her sleeve. She was to busy running the strip club she had opened, to launder money thru, the to be concerned with heartbreak. She distributed large amounts of Coke thru her club, washing her money thru the business as well. She was a good mother to her nine year old daughter. Monica never looked at Zayley as a threat. She knew she was the one who would always have Martrons back. She had her own money. Zayley on the other hand hadn't built anything outside of Martron. If he left her she would be broken down. " What's good with you Mon? Where you at with it? On my way to get Marshaylee from her baby sitter. Monica I told you about having my daughter everywhere. You need

to stay you're ass at home sometimes. She's with

my little cousin. Calm down I'm not even going

into the club tonight. I had to hold some auditions.

Marshaylee is having a sleep over tonight. Is that

right? I was hoping to talk to her. Don't trip she's

good. Some little nigga call himself liking our

baby. I told his 12 year old ass to stay away from

our baby. You don't play no games Mon, He's to

old for her. He's a young white boy. Your daughter

love her a little cute white boy" Martron figured as

much; Monica lived In a eight bedroom house in

Baldwin hills she had black neighbors. Politicians

some retired celebrities. She also lived around a

lot of elite white people. " Monica I love you for holding shit down, I know you do. Tia doing all this dumb shit. Imma need you to come out here to look out for her baby when she has him. Martron what about the club? You can hire someone to manage it. I want you too bring Marshaylee too. Are you sure? Yes I'm fo sho going to make sure everything is set up by the time she goes into labor. Tia isn't ready to be nobody's mother." Monica was sharp she knew her baby's father would put a few niggas to sleep, before he had her and his daughter come to Oregon. They were each other's true best friends. Monica was a loyal women, they could never be together because she would never be the women he wanted her to be. She was okay with that, she had a few guys she dealt with. Monica wanted Martron happy even if they were not together. He was a good father to their daughter that was what meant the most to her. No matter their differences or the differences he had with Zayley he was always a active father. He had told her about Cynthia she knew she was a threat to the young girl because she was indeed a boss. Monica did not want Martron she was okay with him being with other women. Martron heard a knock at his car window. It was Lamar. "Nigga get in the car. What's good with you?what you doing over here? Buying some tree from the

373

hommie. I can't wait to have this meeting Mar Ru.

Yes man It's a few things we need to take care of.

Okay well we can discuss details in front of the

hommies. You look ready to lay somebody down

right now. Dressed in all that damn black. I'm

always ready for whatever. We might as well head

to your house now. We can smoke and chop it up

and shit." Lamar got out of the Range Rover

getting Into his Hummer truck. They drove to

Lamars house. The two home boys hung out for a

few hours . Their other homeboys arrived.

Sleepless, Hennessy, C.K Leon, Value and their

youngest homeboy in their circle Lil' Rich. Martron

smiled as he greeted his partners he knew bullets

would fly, pistols would clap on his enemies.

Lamar sat on the porch with Casey they smoked a

blunt. She was overjoyed, loving when her little

homeboys came over. None of the young men were

over the age 26. They entered the basement.

Which was decked out with a pool table, Play

station 2, hooked up to a 72 inch T.V, white

leather Sofia's decorated In red, black and white

pillows. The walls were adorned with pictures of

different scenes of Al Pacino in Scarface. Each

photo was poster size black white with red writing.

There was a fire place dedicated to the dead

hommies, several pictures were plastered over the

fireplace of fallen soldiers with the Lord's Prayer

in scriptorial writing beside the pictures. Red and black candles were lined up on top of the fire place. Martron took a stance In the middle of the floor. He spoke assertively to the small crowd. " I know y'all wonder why I called this meeting. Well when I was o.t laying low Madrix violated me to the max. That nigga started pimping on my lil' sister Tia and got her pregnant. I feel like he needs to be exed off for the shit he did to my sister, bodied to be exact. The nigga David gotta go, for the shit he did to Ronnie. We can't take that shit light. We can't move sloppy. Them Hoover niggas ain't coming to play. They will lay any weak link down easily and y'all know that! Lastly Its some out of town nigga pimping my sister now. She five

months pregnant on drugs and shit. The nigga

name Charlie Way. He brown skin, lanky and got a

philly hair cut. He post to be a Cali nigga. I called

this meeting because I ride for the hood In every

way and I've put in so much work."

Everybody nodded their heads but Sleepless. He

spoke In a rough tone. " Madrix is my homeboy it

ain't our fault your lil sister Is a crab ass hoe bitch.

Plus I heard she set the nigga Kevin up. None of

that is our problem. I'm not riding against my

homeboy." Nobody saw it coming Martron was

known for doing the unexpected . He removed his

45. Caliber gun from his waist. Sleepless was

sitting on the edge of the pool table. Martron put three bullets into his head. The concrete walls were covered in brain matter. Sleepless lifeless body twitched as it hit the concrete floor. The other bloods fell silent. Casey spoke " Niggas like Sleepless have no respect, Mar Ru is our homeboy . And we gonna ride for him. I had love for Sleepless but he just violated the hommie. We take no disrespect when it comes to family. And if any of y'all disrespect I'll body you niggas myself." Sleepless body was placed in C.K Leon's trunk. He was to get rid of the body. He knew how to dispose of a corpse well. The streets were hot. Summer would begin with a high murder rate.

Tia took had taken her braids out. She washed ,

blow dried and flat Ironed her hair. Her watch

read 4:00 pm. She had two hours to make It to her

visit with Cynthia. She had forty missed calls from

Charlie. He wasn't the focus of her day. She was

only concerned with her visit with Cynthia. She

yearned for a hit of cocaine. Tia snorted two lines

of the powder substance, it made her feel ampted

up. Tia left the hotel at 5:30 pm. She arrived at

Coffee Creek Correctional Facility at 6:10 pm. She

was led into the visiting room. By a female officer

who appeared to be manly. The correctional

officer was layed back. Tia was surprised. " Ms.

Brandt, inmate Richardson should be here shortly

379

take a seat." The C.O was layed back. The visiting room Sargent was not. He was a Hispanic man. Staring at Tia as If she was a criminal. Tia didn't pay the man any mind. She consumed vending machine snacks. Cynthia arrived after Tia waited for fifteen minutes. Prison gave Cynthia glow. She was still beautiful. Wearing her natural hair in wrap, with side bangs, Cynthia always had long hair but it had grown down her back. Her light skin tone gleamed. She wore light green eyeshadow and lip gloss. Her stomach was extremely flat. Her shape was perfect in the D.O.C issued clothes. The Navy blue blue T-shirt with inmate largely printed on the back side in orange writing fit her snuggly. Her breast were perky in the shirt. She wore prison blue jeans with the same orange emblem on the right pants leg. Cynthia wore white Nike Track shoes. Once Cynthia reached chair number 15, Tia stood. The two friends hugged for nearly a full minute. Both of the young women started to cry. They both took their seats in the plastic visiting chairs. "Damn Tia I miss you. You are so skinny! I expected you to be much bigger. How far along are you bitch? Six months next week. Damn I can't believe you are pregnant tell me everything. We got until nine a clock. I will after you tell me what you want me to get out the machines. I want some pretzels and orange soda. That's all you want? Yes girl my drawer is full of food. Your brother keeps my books fat I stay grubbing." Tia came back to the table with what Cynthia asked for. " So how are you Cyn? I'm okay, I work in the kitchen here it's disgusting. I'm a dish washer. My mom comes to visit me a lot. So I'm barley in that stank ass kitchen. I go to church almost everyday. I swear if it wasn't for gods grace I'd be miserable In here. I work out six days a week. Girl you see how much better my shape has got. I do girl you look so good. Thank you, I read a lot of books, more then anything I pray. And hang with a few local bitches In here.Who In here with you Cynthia? Iesha

Martin and Nicole Freeman. You kicking it with them ghetto ass hood rats? Tia was shocked the names Cynthia mentioned did not have good reputations on the streets. "Yes girl them bitches is cool. We may have never kicked it on the streets but they hella cool. We are going they the same thing doing this time. It's good to have people rock with you. I have never been to prison. But I see where you're coming from when you put it like that." Tia shifted in her seat, she was in need of a hit of cocaine.

A hour into the visit, the room started to crowd. Tia could barely hear herself think. She wanted to express all her issues to Cynthia. Tia decided to hold back some. Due to the other visitors sitting Fairly close to them. She also wonders if Cynthia would continue to be her friend if she told her what life she was living. " So girl you said your baby is by Madrix how did that happen? Cynthia there's so much I have to tell you. But I really don't want, or need you to be judging me bitch. Tia began to cry, she had allowed herself to be broken down while her dear friend was away in prison. It was against visiting rules to touch. Cynthia saw that her friend was in pain. She grabbed Tias right hand holding It in a firm grip. Cynthia cupped Tias hand with the both of hers. Holding it as if she was a small child. Cynthia looked her best friend in the eye with sincerity.

"Tia I would never judge you for anything you do. You are a part of me you are my ace. When one of us go thru it we both go thru it." Tia knew Cynthia was being honest. She had been thru a lot before her time in prison, Tia always felt her friends pain.

"Okay Cyn so much has happened since you ruined your life for my brother. Bitch you just told me not to judge you but you judging me how did I ruin my life?" Tia had let the drugs do the talking for her. She put Cynthia down to make herself feel better.

"Bitch you come in here judging me because I wasn't letting my nigga do five to ten when I could do this baby ass time." Tia fidgeted In her chair, she looked down at the table. " The reason I think Madrix is my sons father is because. I started sleeping with him the night you got shot. I was vulnerable from losing my mom and he was there for me.Martron left me for dead going to Cali. You ended up In the county, Kevin was shot up, my dad ain't never been a dad and my mom died. Madrix spoiled me and loved me. Tia that's not a big deal your brother can't be mad because of Madrix age but he was the only one there for you. Cyn that's not it. I saw Kevin on my sweet 16. He was on some let's get back right shit. But I hella dissed him because I was already fucking with Madrix. I know Kevin really did love me." Tia started to shed more tears, she cried uncontrollably. The laid back C.O gave Tia a full roll of toilet paper for the table. Tia dabbed her face; she wanted to be strong but she couldn't find the strength. "Okay Cynthia let me finish telling you. After I clowned Kevin me and Madrix left to Vegas. I'm ashamed that I let him turn me out. That pervert ass nigga had you hoen Tia?So your dad was right? He kept telling your brother that's what he thought all along." Cynthias voice elevated octaves. " Aight Cynthia there's hella people in here. Calm down, how am I post to calm down hearing some shit like that? Fuck It finish telling me the damn story. Well I was getting money with Madrix. A lot of it and honestly Cyn it's easy ass work I loved it. He had me working with two other chicks. Mahogany and Snow, them bitches Is about they paper. They showed me how to really get money. Martron called Madrix one day deciding he was coming home. We flew home tryna play it off. That's when my bro got hit. My ass was so dramatic thinking Martron was gonna die. That I passed out. That's when I found out I was pregnant bitch. Girl I had the clap too. So Tia you was bare backing Madrix nasty ass? You know he had to be fucking Veda and probably his other hoes too. You don't know how them bitches was getting down. Girl I never thought about none of that. But I did start fucking with powder. Madrix hoes got me addicted to the shit. I'm just like my mom a hod and a dope fiend." Cynthia was saddened by the things Tia was telling her. Her friend was worst off then her and she was free. " Tia you can get into treatment. You don't have to use drugs man. It's no good for the baby. I can't stop I got raped when I was hoen in Atlanta, Cyn you don't know the shit that has happened to me. I was stuck out there I had been fucking with Madrix but I didn't want to throw him under the bust when I went to the hospital. The police showed up and shit so I lied like I was visiting a school friend. I had no choice but to call my dad. When he came this nigga wanted to suddenly be a father because he had a new bitch

R.I.P That's a whole nother story but what I'm

saying is. I can't stop using drugs. I need them

now everything bad has happened to me. I went to

jail for a few days and all." Cynthia cried for her

friend. Tia had taken the wrong path. Although

her mother was a hoe herself. She had done her

best to keep Tia away from the lifestyle. It was

heartbreaking for Cynthia to watch her friend fail.

" Tia I love you, your dad loves you , Kevin loves

you, your brother loves you go home. How do you

know I haven't been around Cyn? Because I talk to

your brother everyday. He never said shit about

you doing drugs but he did figure out about

Madrix being your pimp. I told him you thought

you was pregnant by the nigga. Why would you

tell my brother that? I told you not to say shit.

Because why would you be pregnant by a grown

ass man and you're only 16 Tia? My brother grown

too and you fucking on him! And I'm done with

Madrix I'm with this new nigga name Charlie Way.

Is he pimping you out too Tia? We are getting

money together! What is he doing to get money?

He's a hustler Cynthia and so am I. Tia he's using

you the nigga don't give a fuck about you. Any

Man that will pimp on a 16 year old pregnant girl

don't give a fuck about nobody." Tia stood up

from her seat she had gone into a coke rage. "Tia

sit down before they say something and lower your tone in here. I'll sit down bitch but I'm starting to think you're a hater. Your mad about niggas loving me because your locked the fuck up. I'm out here getting money. Tia any nigga that will sale you to strangers to keep his pockets up don't give a damn about you. Don't you feel empty every time you touch a trick? No bitch I feel like I'm getting my money. Don't you feel empty when you go to sleep In a cold ass cell at night. Bitch you free but you in prison within, Im free in my soul bitch! You're a fucking jail bird Cyn! Rather be that then a coke whore bitch. Tia stormed out of the visiting room. She didn't even look back at

Cynthia. If she did she would haul off and slap her. She didn't want to go to jail she wanted to do some coke. She got Inside her rental car pulling out the prison parking lot. Two miles outside of the prison. Tia pulled over to the side of the road, braking down three lines of cocaine she snorted them off her makeup compact. Tia didn't even use a straw or rolled up piece of money, snorting all the drug up her nose.

Chapter 17

Martron and his homeboys were on the hunt they had frequented strip clubs every night of the week. Martron thought they would be able to spot either Madrix or Charlie Way in strip country recruiting a hoe, or two. They had heard the Hoover's would

be at the Stars Cabaret in Beaverton Oregon.The

agenda was to find Madrix or Charlie Way, David

dying would be acceptable as well. Lil' Rich drove

a Chevy Sedan. His homeboys occupied the Sedan

They pulled into the parking lot in the vehicle,

which had to tinted windows. They were all

heavily armed . Paying the bouncer at the front

door to be let in with their weapons. The Pirus

were not inside the club for more then five minutes

when shots started to ring. They had been spotted

by the Hoover's. Lil' Rich was the first one to get

hit. He was struck by a glock 16. Shot in his neck.

Chocking on his own blood while he layed on the

floor. Lamar was hit next in his head from the bullet of a 380. He collapsed to the ground quickly. Martron ducked and covered they were outnumbered by far. Hennessy and Value did the same thing. They had just watched two of their friends die. David was on the front line. He had used the gun that killed Lamar. Martron sprayed bullets as he tucked behind the table of the club. His cohorts followed. They made it outside the club. As they got into the van. Hennessy was also shot to death. Two bullets to his chest took him out. They had went with a mission in mind and failed terribly. Martron was not thinking straight. He knew he should had came with more of his homies.He knew the Hoover's were dangerous. He

had lost that battle. He yelled while Value drived.

" Blood how In the fuck we let them snoove niggas

do us like that." Value didn't respond He only

cried. Lil' Rich was his younger brother he had

failed his mother by being present when his

brother died. Martron was upset that C.K Leon was

not there when the drama occurred. He had still

been on his job he called Matron with news. "

Blood I think I'm looking at the Cali nigga up here

at the Boom Boom room, for real you sure it's

him? Hell yeah the nigga was talking to a Latin

stripper bitch he said his name Is Charlie Way.

Okay blood Im on my way." Martron had Value

drop him off to his Range Rover that he parked at Lamars house. He told Value to tell Casey the news and to get rid of the sedan. He wanted to speak with her, but he had other beef to attend to. Martron parked outside of the strip club on Babur Blvd. Waiting for Charlie Way to leave. C.K Leon texted him everything Charlie Way was wearing. He wore a tan Gucci hat, a Gucci polo shirt. Light blue Encye' Jeans and tan Gucci loafers. He rocked an iced out White gold Rolex on his risk. He was definitely noticeable. Martron sat outside the club for an hour and a half. Long behold the brown skin man dressed in Gucci stepped out of the Strip club. Charlie Way got inside a Black BMW rental car. Martron tailed behind him. Charlie Way

noticed he was being followed. He made multiple

turns until he turned into a dead end. Charlie had

a revolver snub nose in his pocket. He pulled it out

ready to confront the person following him. He

stepped out of the BMW. He was immediately

struck in his right calf with a bullet. Causing him to

fall to the gravel in the dead end he had turned

on. Martron had great aim. He had shot Charlie by

rolling his window down, and sticking his arm out.

Martron stepped out of his vehicle. Walking up to a

screeching Charlie Way. He looked at the man

suffering. Charlie Way had dropped the revolver

when he fell. It was raining hard outside. The

weather caused the gun to slide away from Charlie Ways reach. Martron stood over the man. He chuckled, taking a blade out of his pocket he took Charlie's jeans down. The pimp pissed himself. He didn't once try to fight back, although his arms were free. He didn't try to fight , he just layed there in shock that he had been shoot. He had taken so many lives. When it came to his life being in danger. He couldn't protect himself. Martron took the blade he sliced Charlie Ways dick off as quickly as he could. Cutting thru the thick skin near the shaft all the around to the front of his penis. Charlie yelled in pain. "Why are you doing this to me? Who are you? Nigga you thought you could come to my city and pimp on my little sister nigga it don't work like that. Martron tied Charlie Way up with a bungee cord he had in case of a car emergency He placed him In the trunk of the Beamer he had driven. Martron sliced Charlie ways throat. Watching him bleed out until he took his last breath.

Tia sat in Down Town Portland searching for a coke dealer. She usually got all of her drugs from Charlie way. Not having her own plug on the drug made it difficult for her to cop. Tia was a bit green to the drug game. She did know that China town in downtown Portland was called the bricks. She had heard her brother talk about making moves there.

She had sat in her hotel room for two hours after

the horrible visit she had with her best friend. She

ran out of Coke and could not reach Charlie. She

did think of going to the bricks to cop some coke.

Tia saw young hooded men and women. Doing

drug exchanges. All she saw were hustlers and

walking zombies. She didn't want to approach any

of the hustlers. She as afraid that one of them

might know Martron. Tia saw a man that looked to

be in his mid 20's hustling his ass off. He wore a

black hoodie, black jeans and black Jordan 1's .

He was not flashy, he didn't want to be seen. Tia

watched him from her rental car. The man was

having a heated conversation in his razor flip

phone when Tia got out the car. She stepped up to the man. " Lil'mama why are you walking up on me like that. I ain't no trick." The man thought Tia was trying to proposition him for sex by the way she walked. "Oh no I'm not on any of that. I'm trying to find some powder. I only sale hard, I sale rocks I don't sale coke." Tia didn't understand the D-Boys lingo. He saw the puzzled look on her face. " I sale crack baby, nigga I ain't no damn crack head. Well if you ain't buying no rocks get the fuck out of my face. I don't smoke crack nigga I already said that. Well why you still standing here? The only other Ingredient in the rocks is baking soda." The D- Boy lied making light of how serious smoking crack really was. "So does the crack feel like how powder feel? I don't know baby I sale dope I don't fuck with either."Tia was jonsing, she heard what crack did to people. She knew she wasn't them. She was a boss bitch in her own eyes. She hoed and got money. Tia thought to herself. "Let me just try this until I can get a powder connect." Tia stood with her hand on her hip talking to the D-Boy. "Can I get 200 dollars worth of the rocks?" The D-boy handed Tia a quote of the crack cocaine. She got Into the rental car, Tia didn't know much about crack, she did know it was smoked in a pipe. She placed two of the crack rocks In her weed pipe. Sucking the pipe while lighting it. The feeling was beyond cocaine. She

felt bells ring in her head. Tia felt like she was on

another planet. She consumed all the crack she

purchased within two hours. Returning to the

block. Finding the same D- Boy she bought twice

as more crack. Tia eventually withdrew $1000

from her bank account buying more crack. She

didn't bother getting back in her rental car. She

smoked the pipe outside in cold rain.

Chapter 18

Tia had ran out of the money she had saved

within three days. She spent $7500 dollars on

crack. She didn't eat, she didn't sleep she smoked

crack. When she ran out of money she sold the

rental car that didn't belong to her. She sold all her clothes and jewelry. She sold her phone, when she had nothing left she sold her Pussy for crack. She became a full fledge Strawberry. Her youthful beauty quickly faded away. The summer had come getting the best of the pregnant teenager.The rain had taken a break In her city. Tia stood, high out of her mind outside a bar in china town . When a puddle appeared under her feet. She was too high to notice. Another addict pointed It out to her. Her water had broken. Tia was in active labor. A young hustler saw what was happening. His mother was a crack head he was a crack baby. He felt for the unborn child. He offered her a ride to the hospital. The hustler merged on to Naito Park

Way. Where he eventually got on the freeway

headed to OHSU hospital. "Look lady I don't know

you. But you really need to lay off the pipe. Give

that baby a chance please." Tia didn't respond her

high was wearing off. The affects of the

contractions were bothering her. Tia stepped

inside the hospital alone. The nurse at the nurse

station had saw the same story plenty of times. A

drug addicted mother, going Into premature

labor.Tia was rushed directly to a delivery room.

While she was in labor she filled out forms . She

had her nurse contact her father and brother. D-

Loc and Martron arrived In labor and delivery.

When they entered the hospital room.Tias back
was hunched over. She sat criss crossed the
anesthesiologists was about to give her a epidural.
Martron had saw his babies mothers get a epidural
. He stopped the anesthesiologists from injecting
the needle. "Excuse me can me and my dad hold
my sisters shoulders please. Yes that is fine"
Martron held one shoulder while D-Loc held the
other. Once the epidural procedure was finished.
Tia was in labor for 4 hours. She was Instructed to
push, She did two series of pushes. Her father held
one of her legs. While her brother held her
shoulder. The baby's small head came out first,
then his small shoulders, his body followed.

Martron and Dloc were so happy the baby was born alive and not stillborn. " Tia what are you going to name My nephew? Symbah Martron Brandt. Tias son was born weighing 3 pounds 2 ounces on July 5th 2005.

Tia and the newborn baby were moved to the intensive care unit. The child would have to be in a incubator. He had to be over five pounds to leave the hospital. Tia didn't ask many questions. She jones to get high. Martron questioned the doctors. " What is exactly wrong with my nephew? The little peanuts lungs are not fully developed. He also was not receiving enough nutrients inside the womb. We have to keep him here until he is over five pounds . We have ran some test finding cocaine in his system. We also have to give him medication to ween him off of the drug." Martron had no idea Tia was using coke. He would be more surprised to find out she was using crack. Once the doctor left he room Martron grilled Tia.

"Bitch I don't give a fuck that you just had the baby. What the fuck was you doing getting high pregnant? Martron get the fuck out of her face son, she just had the damn baby. I messed with coke here and there what's the big fucking deal." Martron wanted to choke Tia. "The big deal is they will take your son from you dummy. Well If that's what they try to do then they can try it. I bet I get him back." D-Loc was tired of Tias constant drama. He knew if worst came to worst Martron would have to have Zayley or Monica get custody of the baby. D-Loc looked Tia Into her eyes. " I may not have been the best father. But the day you were born was one of the best days of my life. When I saw you had your mamas eyes I just cried. Your mom hustled most her pregnancy with you. But you still came out big and strong. You were healthy baby. Your mom wasn't using no dope back then. Tia I love you and I just want you to do better for baby Symbah." The conversation was Interrupted by a knock at the room door. In

410

walked in a Italian man In a grungy suit. "You guys the Brandt family? Yes we are." D-Loc spoke knowing a man in a suit asking questions wasn't good news. "I'm detective Vernelli'. I came here today because we believe we found a suspect In the murder of Nyemiah. A man named Johnny Wayne Thompson. D-Loc was shocked but didn't show it. How do you figure that?" Martron inquired. "During the investigation we sent Nyemiahs Lap top to a UfED center . All of the data from her lap top was downloaded. It was all abstracted saved to a hard drive. We discovered, multiple romantic photos of the late Ms. Gibson and Mr. Thompson. There were also several text messages that we were able to retrieve from

downloading the data from her cellphone.The two

were in a heated argument just hours before she

was murdered. We just received the surveillance

from her apartment parking lot. The cameras

show the suspect, enter the apartment twenty

minutes before her death. We tracked the

purchases from his debit card. He had bought

cigarettes a hour before at a chevron gas station.

Johnny Wayne, also purchased heroine from a

known dealer on camera in front of the store. We

tracked down the dealer, threatening him to

charge him with murder. He sang like a Canary.

He said Mr.Thompson was fuming angry, the

dealer said he continued to talk about offing somebody. We know he did it. This will be a easy conviction." Tia, Martron and D-Loc were all shocked. Before they could even discuss the drama. The incubator was wheeled into the room. They all took a good look at the baby. He was a spiting image of Kevin, the only feature he had of Tias was her green eyes. They were all relived the child wasn't Madrix baby. He would still be chastised for his wrong doings. It was a blessing that he wasn't the baby's father. Tia told her dad and her brother she was going to the nurses station to ask for pads. They should had payed more attention to her words vs actions. The nurses waited on new mothers hand and foot. Tia exited

the room finding the nearest elevator. She took it

to the ground floor where she flagged down a cab.

Tia took the cab to the bricks. Her womb was open

from having Symbah, she did not care. She just

wanted to get the monkey off her back. Tia

wanted to get high.

   She ditched the cab running fast. A dealer she

had bought drugs from, saw the altercation. He

reached into his pocket and paid the cabbie.Tia

then went Into a near by alley with the dealer.

Having sex with him after she had given birth only

hours before. Blood clouts ran down the mans

penis as he stroked her in and out. Tia was not

concerned with getting an Infection. She wanted to get high. She was given fifty dollars worth of crack for the encounter.

After the hospital staff realized Tia had left her son. They looked for next to kin. Martron had Monica fly in the very next day. She lied and said D-loc was her father, as a sibling. Monica could have custody of Symbah. She would have to take parenting classes, with him being premature and under weight she had the time to do so.

Chapter 19

Tia stayed downtown smoking crack and exchanging sex for two weeks after she had her son. She smelled of death, yet she could still fuck fellow crack heads for a hit and the dealers. Tia stood by the 76 gas station in China Town. She needed a hit it was 4 am raining in the summer in Portland. None of the dealers were out. A single black Coupe Deville, slid down the street. The car pulled into the gas station. Out stepped a women dressed in nun attire. She walked Into the gas station paid the attendant for her gas and approached Tia. " I see all the pain and tragedy you've bee thru, Bitch get out my face you don't know me. I don't but god does he knows your son needs you to." Tia was thrown off how did the women know she had a son. Tia held her mouth with the palm of her hand. The women Speke softly. "Come with me I can help you.Tia knew the women had to be. A profit of some sort, instead of arguing with the women. Tia got Into the car with her. She drove Tia to South East Portland to an Oxford house. Tia was introduced to the head drug and alcohol counselor Zach. He was a slinder white man, with a Justin Timberlake type of face. He was Indeed Handsome.

He gave Tia a Towel, wash cloth and toiletries. Zach showed Tia were the bathroom was. There she was able to wash her hair, shower and change into the donated sweat suit Zach had given her. Once she was cleaned, Both the nun and Zach spoke to Tia. " you're more then welcome here.

Please don't go, We want to help you." Tia was

placed in a bedroom with two sets of bunks beds.

It was clean neat and spacious. Zach gave her a

notebook. " Tia this Is for journaling you can write

in it at any time, here's a list of the house rules,

Breakfast at 7:30 so please rest up." The time was

6:10am Tia took a nap, telling herself god had sent

her to the treatment center by causing her to meet

the nun, it was surely fate. Tia was in the

treatment center for two weeks, when she

disclosed she had a son. She was too embarrassed

to tell any of the staff or clients about what she

had done to Symbah. Zach helped her get in

contact with her father. D-Loc came right to Tia's

rescue. He wouldn't give up on her. She told her
father the truth in the living room. " Daddy I was
so caught up on the coke that I started smoking, I
know baby your brother asked around. Did he?
yes he did." Tia was wearing a long green maxi
dress tears of shame floated down her face. How
could she become a crack head? Was life that hard
that she could do drugs while she was pregnant
with no remorse? How could she leave her son, her
first born son? Tia thought of so many answers.
Which all led to her being selfish. "I know this is
crazy to ask, but dad where's Symbah? Please
don't tell me he's In foster care. No we would
never let that happen Martron flew Monica out

here she's been at the hospital with that boy day in

and day out . He should be getting out next

week.Thank god my baby is with family." Tia

knew Monica well she had traveled to Oakland

with her brother numerous times to visit her niece

Marshaylee. Tias life was being touched by a

angel. Zach coached her on how to get out of the

cycles of addiction. He had once been strung out

 on heroine, he was a recovering addict.

   Zach recommended Tia do A 90 day treatment

program. He wanted to do his best to guide her to

get off of drugs. Tia was told not to even smoke

weed. She was to not touch any drug. Tia Jones

daily, when she did she would journal. In her one

on one sessions with Zach. Tia spoke about missing Symbah, the guilt she had for using drugs and prostituting while pregnant. " Zach I don't know what the fuck was wrong with me. I was for real lost. I really was just numbing myself and lost out there. Don't beat yourself up Tia. When I was addicted to heroine. I did The worst things to my kids, I left them for dead living in a abandoned car. The state took them from me. I had to clean myself up, to see they were worth living for my life really sucked then. You're so smart Tia go to school pursue your dreams." Zach helped Tia enroll in Portland Community College. She took her placement test receiving high scores. Tia took the General Studies Classes. She hadn't decided on a Major or Minor.

Once Tia was in the treatment program for sixty days. Monica started to bring Symbah to visit her. Tia was overjoyed during every visits. " Hey baby, you're so beautiful. I love you so much my King. Mommy Is so sorry for all the wrong she ever did to you." Tia apologized to her son often he meant the world to her. Symbah was being well taken care of. He had survived all the health issues he previously faced. He was a strong baby boy. He resembled his father Kevin more and more each day. Tia was afraid to reach out to Kevin. She thought he would deny being in her sons life.She didn't want to feel any more rejection. She also didn't want her son to feel rejected. Tia had been thru the hardest part. The first month in treatment was the difficult. Tia had to be in a black out period. Where she was not allowed to leave or have contact with any one. Zach had bent the rules letting her talk to D-Loc. She thought back on it, happy that she had made it out of the black out phase.

Dloc was proud of Tia, she had a 4.0 GPA. She was focusing on her education as she had done when she was in high school. Tia would obtain her degree well before her 21st birthday.

With a clean mind Tia had made up with Cynthia preparing for her best friends return home. Cynthia had entered a treatment program in prison that would give her a earlier release. The two chatted on the phone daily. " Tia bitch I cant wait to get out of this bitch. I know you can't. My mom got me so much new shit imma come out looking good. But my focus is getting out getting me a job and going to school. Your brother told me I don't have to because he will take care of me. But I will never just depend on no nigga. That's smart best friend I feel you." The two girls chatted for a full thirty minute phone call. Ending their conversation with love.

Cynthia was released two weeks before Tias graduation from treatment. Tia received a overnight pass to stay the night with her best friend. Cynthia instantly wanted to party , Tia thought to herself that she was not ready for a Party. She didn't want to be a bad friend to Cynthia by expressing her truth. Tia played off the fact that she feared going to a party. The two girls walked from Cynthias house. To Mississippi and Skidmore. They were attending a party at a apartment located in the corner of the block. They walked up the stairs of the brick apartments. When they entered the doors of the apartment. The ladies were treated like hood celebrities. Tia had snapped back as if she had never been pregnant, Cynthia had a glow from prison. Both of the girls were the center of attention. Cynthia dove right in to consuming liquor. Tia did not want to participate. She stood on the side lines acting bougie. Tia watched Cynthia dance, socialize and have the time of her life. She walked up to Tia confused on her antisocial behavior. " What's up Tia why you acting all stuck up? This ain't the type of crowd I be around bitch. Oh yes my best friend a college girl. I feel it at least dance with me." Tia left the wall stepping on to the middle of the floor. The two friends danced to, Chris Brown "Poping". The R&B artist had taken the game by storm quickly with his debut album. The song blasted

loudly out of the large speakers.

Tia had held her bladder thru the song, needing

to use the restroom. She walked to the bathroom.

Opening the door without knocking. A Asian girl

and a mixed girl, were In the bathroom snorting

lines of cocaine. Tias mouth instantly started to

water. She forgot the urge to urinate, she wanted

to hit the cocaine. The two girls saw the look In

her eyes. The Mixed girl spoke.

"You want some blow Its enough to go around?"

Tia didn't answer she just took the straw out of the

girls hand snorting two pre cut lines of the

cocaine. She had relapsed easily. Tia waited until

she saw Cynthia busy with a conversation, to slide by her and leave out the door of the party.

Tia didn't return to the treatment center. Instead she called Mahogany. Tia hadn't reached out to her when she was raped. Believing if she was In touch with Mahogany, the Atlanta police would some how tie her to Madrix. Tia called Mahogany, "Yo who this? This Tia? Oh my god bitch where have you been? Girl that's way to much to explain but I need to get up out of town? Where's the baby has the baby been born yet? He's with family he's fine. I just really need to get out of Portland."

Mahogany would not continue to question Tia she sent her a airline ticket to Atlanta. When Tia made it back To The A. She didn't feel the way she had felt when she left the city. She was looking for a fresh start. The difference was she had been thru the storm. She just wanted to trap without all the drama. She didn't feign to smoke crack. Tia did want to use cocaine. She knew hanging around Mahogany, she could have full access to getting money and getting high.

Mahogany greeted Tia at the airport with a big hug and a kiss on the lips. They chopped it up as they walked to the baggage claim area. " Tia me and Snow stayed out here. After that shit happened to you and Madrix acted like he didn't give a fuck. We stopped fucking with him. The nigga couldn't protect you. So he couldn't protect us, or anybody at that. I guess the nigga out in Mississippi saling dope. He calls me sometimes looking for a friend. You know Veda was bodied? Yes I heard about that . He says your brother is on his head sucks for him."

Mahogany and Snow lived In Marietta Georgia in a three bedroom house. The home was two stories tall. The home had French Doors leading to each room, large ceilings and plush imported home décor. Snow had gotten all high priced items from Italy. The women finally had full control of their money. They lived comfortably vs. living from hotel to hotel.

Martron was on a rampage because of the lost he took the night at the Stars strip Club. He couldn't keep his cool or handle his business correctly. He was moving sloppy. His DNA had been found On Veda although he wore a condom. She had touched his dick when he removed his pants. Pre Cum sat in her nail bids. There was a warrant for Martrons arrest. Leaving town would be smart, Martron sat in Portland waiting for Madrix to be spotted. He was obsessed with killing him. It would cost him his freedom.

Chapter 20

Mahogany asked Tia to move in. Snow had met a point guard that played for the Houston Rockets.

431

He proposed to her after two months of dating. "Tia you should move in here so Mahogany won't be lonely. I'm changing my life though. When he pulled out this big rock I said yesssssssss.!" Snow flashed bling on her ring finger. She was proudly engaged. Tia envied Snow that she was able to have a fresh start with a man that truly loved her.

A week after Tia arrived Snow moved out to start her new life. Tia moved in fully, Mahogany bought Tia an entire new wardrobe. She had 6 figures worth of money. Planning on getting 7 figures.

D-Loc was stressed out, Martron was on the run. Tia was missing in action again. He kept Symbah due to Monica having to travel back and forth to California to run her business. Martron suggested she sale the club. Monica kept it for financial security. D-Loc sat in his den full of stress when he received the call he didn't want to receive. "You have a collect call from, Mar Ru, to except please press five to disconnect press two or hang up."

D-Loc pressed the number five button. " Whats up Pops? Hey son what's going on? They got me in here on some bullshit. Just do me a favor and get at Tobbie about that thang." D-Loc knew Martron was telling him to take over his operation. He needed him to get In touch with Tobbie the second in command. Martron had got caught up in a routine traffic stop. He sped thru a red light on N.E 42nd and Killingsworth. The officer pulled him over. Quickly Noticing he was on the most wanted list. Martrons picture was blasted all over every Portland police precincts walls.

" Hey I'm over here on 42nd and Killingsworth. I think I got Martron Brandt, issue backup." The officer had stepped away from the car as if he was running the plates. However he was calling backup to the four way stop on Killingsworth to take Martron in. He was considered armed and dangerous. Once apprehended. Three fire arms were found In Martrons Beamer and one on his person. D-Loc stressed the days after he spoke to his son. Hiring him a team of lawyers. Martron would not get out. He had been sloppy with Charlie way as well, his DNA was on the bungee he used to tie Charlie up. Martron was fighting two murders. D-Loc was afraid his son would get the death penalty.

There was a huge party at the Magic city strip club In Atlanta. Mahogany had been out on the VIP list. She urged Tia to go knowing there would be ballers in the building. " Bitch put on the bright pink halter dress hurry up! You already showered come on!" Mahogany wore her hair in a high Jenny ponytail. With a blue, silk, Versace romper. Tia wore a pink Chanel halter dress. They both wore open toed Christian Louis Vu Ton red bottom heels the colors of their outfits.

Mahogany snagged the first nigga she saw with the largest stack in his hand, it wasn't the stack that caught her eye. It was the Tom ford suit he wore, the Rolex he rocked, the VIP section he had and the entourage . Tia was not interested in the man or his friends the crowd was older. Instead Tia walked around the club looking for her own baller. Tia looked around the poping strip club. Surprised when she spotted Kevin. Their eyes locked at the same time. They walked towards each other in the crowded club. When their bodies met the two former lovers hugged for, what felt like forever.

Kevin took her outside to his green Hummer truck to talk. "Tia what are you doing out here? I moved out here. Kevin I had a baby! You had a baby? You let that nigga get you pregnant? No he's your son." Kevin was stunned he had a child he was overjoyed. "Wow do you have any picture of my son?" Tia pulled out her sidekick cell phone. She had several pictures of Symbah on her phone. Kevin started to laugh and cry at the same time. "Tia why would you keep my baby away from me? I was not trying to keep him away from you. I didn't know if you would want anything to do with him! What type of nigga you think I am? Even If me and you are not together , that's still my son. I could never be without my son, I am him and he is me!" Tia didn't even argue with Kevin he was right. She was surprised when he hugged and kissed her. "Tia I still love you! And now I know you gave me a baby. Kevin Ive been thru so much." Tia called Mahogany telling her she was leaving the club. Kevin was a student at Georgia Tech. He took her back to his room where she told him everything she had been thru. He also had information for her. "Tia regarding my dad and your mom. I honestly had no idea. Kevin I know. Well baby since you ain't been in Portland you probably haven't heard? What's up? My dad was caught yesterday in Mexico for the murder of your mom." Tia began to cry, her mothers murder would be solved. It was to close to home. Her sons grandfather had murdered her mother.

Johnny Wayne had drank so many years. That he didn't make it to his preliminary court dates. The O.G died from liver complications in the Clark county jail in Vancouver Washington. Samantha and her sons were surprised that Johnny was worth 6 million dollars from his car dealerships. He spilt the money Among his children and his wife. Tia stayed with Mahogany for a month once she reunited with Kevin. He had her tested for all STDs before he was intimate with her to be safe.

Tia transferred her credits to Clark University where she was accepted. Kevin bought the two of them a home.

Three months later…..

Tia, Kevin, Mahogany Dloc and Monica all sat in the Multnomah County court house . They were in attendance for the custodial rights for Symbah. It was Tias chance to speak. " Hi my name is Tia Jade Brandt. I'm a teenage mother that has made a lot of mistakes. I love my son with all my heart. I take accountability for my drug addiction and the fact that I left my poor baby. I left him at birth to get high. Addiction is real; I am a recovering addict my drug of choice was cocaine as well as Crack cocaine, weed, ecastcy and alcohol .I quit every substance cold turkey. I'm attending Clark University. I have a 4.0 GPA, I currently live with my fiancé in Decatur Georgia. Kevin Is Symbah biological father. He was not aware I had my son until three months ago we are engaged and financially capable of taking care of our son. I completed oxford treatment in Atlanta. I graduated the drug and alcohol program. I am now In school to become a drug and alcohol counselor myself. If you give me the rights to my son. I promise to give him a great life." Tias drug and alcohol counselors and her professors spoke on her behalf on speaker phone."

Tia and her family sat for a hour in the courtroom gallery. The judged returned with a verdict. " Ms. Brandt you and your fiancé are granted full custody of Symbah Brandt. Take care of that baby." Tia could cry, she was to happy to cry. She had been thru the storm. She was finally wining in life. Kevin and Tia returned to Georgia. Where they held their son together. 16 year old Tia Jade Brandt held her son with her finance. His green eyes blinked at the blue sky with grey contrast.

The End

Epilogue

2007...... Martron had got off with a light sentence. The power of money helped him get 25 years. That was a low sentence compared to all the dirt he had done. He sat In the Oregon's Federal holding jail, Columbia County.

Martron had been indicted on petty drug charges from saling drugs in county jail while he fought his case. He sat calmly on the phone with Tia. " You think you so tight becausee you married that nigga! Leave me alone, nah Kevin is cool, how's my little nephew doing? He's doing great. How are you bro? Still getting to this money fighting these bullshit charges. Well bro god got you. Kevin just walked in I'm gonna start dinner. Okay tell him I said what's up. I will." Martron hung up the phone Returning to his cell, he sat on his bunk reading a new hood book by the author "Nicki Turner". His reading was interrupted by the noise he heard coming from the day room. New inmates were arriving. Martron laid his eyes on Madrix. He quickly went to his bunk grabbing a jail house shank he had made. Martron waited for the cell doors to open for entry to the day room. He had saw what cell Madrix was escorted to which was located on the bottom tier with him. Madrix hadn't saw Martron nor knew he was being housed at Columbia County Jail. Martron entered Madrix cell.

As the new inmate made his bunk. Martron crept

up on him. Madrix was met by the shank going

into his ribs. Martron stabbed his former best

friend 13 times. " Nigga I really loved you. But all

busta ass niggas get got!If they fuck with a

Brandt."

Madrix lifeless body dropped to the ground.

Stay tuned the streets were just heating up in

"Dead Roses", "Roses Are Blue" will show you

who really holds down the crown in the streets of

Portland.

Roses Are Blue

Tiffany sat In the dark basement close to

Unconsciousness . How could she let herself get

caught up In the bullshit the streets had to offer?

She thought of her dead parents and her sister

Aujanique. She knew she would see them soon.

The stench of urin and feces filled her nostrils. She

had been In the horrific basement for three days.

However It felt like three years.

   All she could think about was her mistakes. "God

I know I haven't talked to you a lot and I've done

a lot of bad things in the door game. But please

forgive me. If you give me one more chance. I will never sale another drug in my life……………..

"Roses are red, Violets are blue, power shifts in a city near you,Martron had the game on lock, but had to do life, Tiffany Is that bitch that came up over night, She wasn't a blood and she did not groove, She was a Crip queen pin and Roses are blue.

Made in United States
Troutdale, OR
07/08/2024